BLACK NO MORE

GEORGE S. SCHUYLER (1895–1977), a satirist, critic, and eminent African American journalist of the Harlem Renaissance, was born in Providence, Rhode Island. After a seven-year stint in the army, he moved to New York City, where he joined the staff of *The Messenger,* the official magazine of the Friends of Negro Freedom, a black socialist group. His writing for *The Messenger* caught the eye of H. L. Mencken, who became a mentor figure to Schuyler; Schuyler soon began writing for Mencken's *The American Mercury,* as well as *The Nation, The Washington Post,* and the *Pittsburgh Courier,* black America's most influential newspaper. He became the first black journalist to attain national prominence and was known for his controversial opinions. In addition to *Black No More,* Schuyler published the novel *Slaves Today* as well as several novellas and an autobiography.

DANZY SENNA is the author of the novels *New People, Symptomatic,* and *Caucasia,* a national bestseller that won the Stephen Crane Award for Best New Fiction and the American Library Association's Alex Award and was translated into nearly a dozen languages. A recipient of the Whiting Writers Award, Senna is also the author of the memoir *Where Did You Sleep Last Night?* and the story collection *You Are Free.* She lives in Los Angeles, where she is a professor of English at the University of Southern California.

GEORGE S. SCHUYLER

Black No More

BEING AN ACCOUNT OF THE STRANGE AND
WONDERFUL WORKINGS OF SCIENCE IN
THE LAND OF THE FREE, A.D. 1933–1940

Introduction by
DANZY SENNA

PENGUIN BOOKS

PENGUIN BOOKS

An imprint of Penguin Random House LLC
375 Hudson Street
New York, New York 10014
penguin.com

First published in the United States of America by The Macaulay Company 1931
This edition with an introduction by Danzy Senna published in Penguin Books 2018

LIBRARY OF CONGRESS CATALOGING-IN-PUBLICATION DATA
Names: Schuyler, George S. (George Samuel), 1895–1977, author.
Title: Black no more / George S. Schuyler ; introduction by Danzy Senna.
Description: New York : Penguin Classics, 2018.
Identifiers: LCCN 2017043210 (print) | LCCN 2017046751 (ebook) |
ISBN 9781524705749 (ebook) | ISBN 9780143131885 (softcover) | ISBN 9781524705749 (ebook)
Subjects: LCSH: African Americans—Fiction. | Human skin color—Fiction. |
BISAC: FICTION / African American / General. | FICTION / Literary. |FICTION / Satire. |
GSAFD: Picaresque literature. | Humorous fiction. | Satire.
Classification: LCC PS3537.C76 (ebook) | LCC PS3537.C76 B56 2018 (print) |
DDC 813/.52—dc23
LC record available at https://lccn.loc.gov/2017043210

Printed in the United States of America
3   5   7   9   10   8   6   4   2

*This book is dedicated
to all Caucasians in the great republic
who can trace their ancestry
back ten generations
and confidently assert that there are no
Black leaves, twigs, limbs, or branches on
their family trees*

Contents

BLACK NO MORE

Introduction

The first time I read George Schuyler's 1931 novel, *Black No More*, it confused and unsettled me. I was in college at the time and not quite ready for its cynical, almost misanthropic vision of race and society.

I had just reached that stage of racial identity that psychologist William Cross, in his 1971 "Negro-to-Black Conversion Experience," called "immersion." The immersion stage (number three of five) is when you eat, drink, and excrete blackness. It's when you bite off the head of anybody who questions whether you, no matter how high your yellow, are anything less than Afrika Bambaataa.

What unsettled me about *Black No More* wasn't just what I knew of Schuyler's vaguely messed-up politics (which became a whole lot less vague and a whole lot more messed up in the decades following the novel's publication). It was also that Schuyler was so merciless—about everyone. At the exact moment I was finding power and purpose in my black identity, he was telling me race didn't exist.

His stance was familiar to me. The truth was, he reminded me of my father, another black intellectual who was prone to making fun of everyone. It was my father who taught me how to laugh at race. As a child, I had already noticed that the discussion of race in white liberal America was always and only a discussion of blackness, never whiteness. In that space of earnestness, blackness became either magical or noble or tragic or essentially wicked. But in the black space of my father's home, race was a far more multilayered conversation. Whiteness was named. Nothing was sacrosanct.

It was my father who told me the first racist jokes I'd ever heard—jokes written by white people at our expense. My father never laughed so hard as he did at those punch lines. Looking back, I think he was trying to teach me the art of black satire—showing me how to find the joke about whiteness hidden within a joke about blackness. I learned from my father how horror could become humor and all the ways humor could be horrifying. What I recognized in reading *Black No More* was a similar sense of the black absurd. But I was in college, three thousand miles from my original home and newly adrift, searching for a place to call home. Schuyler thumbed his nose at the very things I was trying to hold sacred.

I squirmed most while reading the chapter in which Schuyler takes down all those Black History Month heroes, especially his lampoon of Marcus Garvey. At eight years old I briefly attended an experimental Afrocentric school based on Garvey's teachings—a miserable experience—but still, I wasn't ready for Schuyler's wicked rendering of the Garveyesque figure he renames Santop Licorice. Mr. Santop Licorice, Schuyler writes, had "for some fifteen years . . . been very profitably advocating the emigration of all the American Negroes to Africa. He had not, of course, gone there himself and had not the slightest intention of going so far from the fleshpots, but he told the other Negroes to go." Schuyler demonstrates here, and throughout the novel, an awareness of the class politics of racial consciousness, writing of the way racial identity politics, like anything else, can become part of the capitalist production wheel:

Naturally the first step in their going [back to Africa] was to join [Licorice's] society by paying five dollars a year for membership,

ten dollars for a gold, green and purple robe and silver-colored
helmet that together cost two dollars and a half, contributing five
dollars to the Santop Licorice Defense Fund (there was a perpetual
defense fund because Licorice was perpetually in the courts for
fraud of some kind). . . . [Licorice attempted] to save the Negroes
by vicariously attacking all of the other Negro organizations and
at the same time preaching racial solidarity and cooperation in
his weekly newspaper, *"The African Abroad,"* which was printed
by white folks and had until a year ago been full of skin-whitening
and hair-straightening advertisements.

Schuyler doesn't stop with Garvey. He pokes fun at James
Weldon Johnson, the high-yellow Harlem Renaissance race-
man who wrote that classic of tragic mulatto literature, *The
Autobiography of an Ex-Colored Man*—and also wrote that
song "Lift Every Voice and Sing," otherwise known as the
black national anthem, which I sang in a quavering voice
every week with my fellow Black Student Union members to
close out our meetings.

Schuyler's most intense vitriol, however, is reserved for
W. E. B. Du Bois, who can easily be recognized in the character of Dr. Shakespeare Agamemnon Beard, founder of the
National Social Equality League. "For a mere six thousand
dollars a year," Schuyler writes of Beard,

the learned doctor wrote scholarly and biting editorials in *The
Dilemma* denouncing the Caucasians whom he secretly admired
and lauding the greatness of the Negroes whom he alternately
pitied and despised. In limpid prose he told of the sufferings and
privations of the downtrodden black workers with whose lives
he was totally and thankfully unfamiliar. Like most Negro leaders, he deified the black woman but abstained from employing
aught save octoroons. He talked at white banquets about "we of
the black race" and admitted in books that he was part-French,
part-Russian, part-Indian and part-Negro. . . . In a real way, he
loved his people.

———————

Black No More is based on a fantastical, speculative premise: What if there were a machine that could turn black people permanently white? What if such a machine were invented in and introduced to 1920s America, a time of both increasing racial pride and persistent racial violence? What would the social and political implications be of such a race-reversal machine? What would it reveal about society? What lies and hypocrisies about blackness and whiteness and American identity would be revealed by the chaos that would ensue?

The protagonist of *Black No More*, Max Disher, has no moral center: He is willing to do anything for personal gain. He is a black man who is so hungry for all that white America has withheld from him that when given the opportunity to turn white, he jumps at the chance to go in the Black-Off machine (a precursor to Dr. Seuss's Star-Off Machine in *The Sneetches*)—as does all of Harlem. They want access to everything that whiteness will afford them: money, freedom, mobility, and power. Like Eddie Murphy in that famous 1980s *SNL* skit "White Like Me," where he dons white pancake makeup and a straight-haired blond wig and goes undercover to discover that white privilege is much worse than he thought, Schuyler's character discovers what he can get in the American marketplace when he is cloaked in a skin tone and bone structure and hair that are read as white. No other novel I've read before or since so baldly exposes whiteness as a valuable commodity.

In the Black-Off machine, Max Disher transforms into Matt Fisher, a white anthropologist. A novel about a black man becomes a novel about a white man who was black once upon a time. And yet while passing into white America, Max-turned-Matt consistently finds only disappointment in the so-called superior race. He mourns his lost blackness, and in doing so reveals the fallacy of white supremacy:

As a boy he had been taught to look up to white folks as just a little less than gods. Now he found them little different from the Negroes, except that they were uniformly less courteous and less interesting. . . . Often when the desire for the happy-go-lucky, jovial good fellowship of the Negroes came upon him strongly, he would go down to Auburn Avenue and stroll around the vicinity, looking at the dark folk and listening to their conversation and banter. But no one down there wanted him around. He was a white man and thus suspect. . . . There was nothing left for him except the hard, materialistic, grasping, ill-bred society of the whites. Sometimes a slight feeling of regret that he had left his people forever would cross his mind, but it fled before the painful memories of past experiences in this, his home town.

Schuyler argued in one of his earlier writings, a 1926 editorial for the *Pittsburgh Courier*, that the roots of white racism were a fear of black superiority. "Whites realize that given free rein, the Negro would very likely be running the country in less than half a century. . . . The average white man of sense knows the average Negro is his equal and very often his superior; that is the reason why he limits the Negro's sphere of activity."

Black No More argues compellingly, provocatively, that the idea of blackness is necessary in order for whiteness to survive. It is much like James Baldwin famously said: "What white people have to do is try and find out in their own hearts why it was necessary to have a nigger in the first place, because I'm not a nigger. I'm a man, but if you think I'm a nigger, it means you need it. . . . If I'm not a nigger and you invented him—you, the white people, invented him—then you've got to find out why. And the future of the country depends on that, whether or not it's able to ask that question."

Schuyler shows all the ways white people are lost without black people to define themselves against. In one late, amazing scene in *Black No More*, the pastor of a failing white church in the South is grieving the loss of black people after they've all turned white. He is grieving the fact that there is nobody left for him to lynch—and without black bodies to lynch, the white parishioners will never know the pastor's true greatness.

Schuyler dedicated *Black No More* to "all Caucasians in the great republic who can trace their ancestry back ten generations and confidently assert that there are no Black leaves, twigs, limbs or branches on their family trees." Before it had been confirmed by social scientists, he understood that there was no such thing as race as a real, biologically determined category. But he saw how real race's influence was, and all the ways racialized thinking—that other opiate of the masses—limited and imprisoned both black and white Americans.

In *Black No More*, racialized thinking has turned white people into nothing but self-satisfied buffoons. The white workers are so distracted by their hatred of black people that they will never see the true source of their oppression, the white wealthy landowners who exploit their labor. Black leaders are portrayed as corrupt—especially the high-yellow octoroons being paid a fortune to speak for the larger race, to whom they feel distant and superior. In one scathing passage Schuyler writes: "While a large staff of officials was eager to end all oppression and persecution of the Negro, they were never so happy and excited as when a Negro was barred from a theater or fried to a crisp." The black and white working classes are shown to be victims of an elite of white supremacists and black racemen who use race as a tool to deflect attention from their own greed.

At a moment when black writers were finally awakening to the beauty of black culture, Schuyler had moved on to the part where we deconstruct race. He showed neither sentimentality nor chauvinism for his own race or any other. He hated everyone, and there is a strange purity to his loathing, a kind of beauty to his cynicism. It is his resistance to pandering, to joining tribes and clubs—to courting today what we might call "likes"—that feels so refreshing. It is the loneliness of Schuyler's position that makes me trust it.

Long before Schuyler published *Black No More*, the seeds of his anti-authority iconoclasm and his impulse toward Swiftian satire had been set in place. He was already disillusioned with every club he had ever flirted with joining.

Schuyler had joined the military as a young, working-class black man and had risen to become a lieutenant, but he defected after a series of racist incidents. Sometime later he arrived in New York City and lived a kind of hobo rogue intellectual life, staying for a time in the Phyllis Wheatley Hotel, owned by Marcus Garvey's Universal Negro Improvement Society—a group he considered joining but whose corruption left a bad taste. He read voraciously all things socialist, and by 1923 he was an editor and columnist for *The Messenger*, a magazine owned by the black socialist Friends of Negro Freedom. But he was already branching out, writing for other publications outside the black press. He published a cutting tongue-in-cheek critique of white supremacy for H. L. Menken's *American Mercury*. In 1926, at the height of the Harlem Renaissance, when Negro life was finally in vogue and Negro culture and art were beginning to be fetishized by both blacks and whites, he wrote a controversial essay for *The Nation* called "The Negro-Art Hokum," in which he criticized romantic primitivism among blacks and whites, famously saying that Negroes were just "lampblacked Anglo-Saxon[s]" and that there was no difference between black and white American culture, only class and geographical differences. A week later Langston Hughes was hired to write a rebuttal; in his essay, "The Negro Artist and the Racial Mountain," he critiqued "this urge within the race toward whiteness, the desire to pour racial individuality into the mold of American standardization, and to be as little Negro and as much American as possible." Hughes argued for a celebration of a distinctly African American aesthetic.

Schuyler's spirit as an outsider was fully in effect. The historian John Henrik Clarke once said of him, "I used to tell people that George got up in the morning, waited to see which way the world was turning, then struck out in the opposite direction." Being a consummate outsider, by force and by choice, left Schuyler free to parody everyone. At the root of his position as a satirist was his cultural homelessness. Though he'd come from working-class roots, he was too well read, well traveled, and successful as a writer to ever return to them. He had no solid home in the black elite either: He was too dark-skinned, for one thing, and lacked pedigree. He chafed against hero worship, orthodoxy, and the glorification of race, and was fascinated by intergroup racism and classism. He married Josephine, a white Texas socialite turned New York bohemian, and they had a baby girl, Philippa. Schuyler's small interracial family became his only tribe—the island of the misfit toys. They lived in Harlem, in the well-to-do black neighborhood of Sugar Hill, where Schuyler published his first novel, *Slaves Today*, which infuriated black America. It was a harsh depiction of Liberia, the oldest black republic in the modern world, founded as a refuge for liberated American slaves. Schuyler depicted the slave trade there as being led by black Africans.

He was a man of contradictions. For someone so utterly unsentimental and sternly rational about race and blackness, he indulged his wife's strange neoessentialist belief in "hybrid vigor"—that is, her belief that their daughter's racial fusion of black and white represented the birth of a new, superior race. With Schuyler's help, his wife turned their only daughter into a social experiment, raising Philippa on a scientifically prepared diet of raw meat, unpasteurized milk, and castor oil, and keeping her in near isolation from other children. The child's strange upbringing was both a raging success and a terrible failure. Philippa learned to read at two, became an accomplished pianist at four, and a composer by five. She was a child celebrity, a kind of black Shirley Temple with a high IQ who became the subject of scores of articles in publications such as *Time*, *The New York Times*, and *The New Yorker*, and was roundly hailed as a genius. There is a poignant moment in Kathryn Talalay's biography of Philippa Schuyler, *Composition in Black and White*, when Philippa is thirteen and her parents finally show her the detailed scrapbook they've been keeping about her upbringing and career—notes and articles they've been keeping diligently over the years. Philippa, rather than being touched, was horrified to realize, with sudden clarity, all the ways she'd been her parents' social experiment and "puppet." In the years that followed, she grew increasingly disillusioned with America, her own blackness, and the musical career of her youth. Like a character out of *Black No More*, she eventually changed her name and began to pass as white—as an Iberian-American named Filipa Montera. She spent most of her adult life overseas, still playing music, but less seriously, and trying to find herself in various romantic affairs. She eventually tried to reinvent herself as an international journalist and children's advocate, and in 1967 she died in a helicopter crash while attempting to evacuate war orphans out of Vietnam.

In the years that followed the publication of *Black No More*, Schuyler's healthy skepticism toward authority and his absurdist, freewheeling humor gave way to rigidity and humorless Far Right extremism. In the end he did join a club, the John Birch Society, and became the kind of tool of the Far Right that he might have brilliantly parodied in his earlier work. The statements he made later in life against the civil rights movement and in particular against Martin Luther King Jr. would taint his public image and allow him to be dismissed as a serious thinker.

The turn against Schuyler can be glimpsed in the 1971 edition of *Black No More*, in the introduction by Charles

Larson, a prominent scholar of African and African American literature. In a scolding, censorious tone, Larson makes it clear how much he dislikes both the novel and its author:

> *Black No More* is disturbing in these days of renewed Black Pride and Black Power. There is no pride in being black and certainly little indication that the black person in America has anything culturally his own worth holding on to. . . . It is a plea for assimilation, for mediocrity, for reduplication, for faith in the (white) American dream. . . . Hardly a page passes by without some aspect of black American life being satirized or attacked. . . . Schuyler's bitterness is clearly apparent.

Reducing *Black No More* to the mildly amusing but ultimately unimportant scribblings of a black reactionary, Larson turns a blind eye to all the ways the novel was and remains a liberating and lacerating critique of American racial madness, capitalism, and white superiority.

Rereading *Black No More* so many years later, in the era of Trump and Rachel Dolezal, Beyoncé's "Formation" and that radical Pepsi commercial starring Kendall Jenner, of the rise and fall of Tiger Woods's land of Cablinasia, and of Michael Jackson's "race lift" and subsequent death, Schuyler's wild, misanthropic, take-no-prisoners satire of American life seems more relevant than ever.

Schuyler belongs to the pantheon of black writers in America who have seen their work either reviled, forgotten, dismissed, or—most commonly—ignored in their own lifetime. In this respect, he belongs in the company of Chester Himes, Fran Ross, William Melvin Kelley, Zora Neale Hurston, and Nella Larsen, most of whom died in poverty or saw their work go out of print, and whose work was appreciated only after they were gone—and in some cases, not yet.

There is no stable ground to stand on in *Black No More*. Its irony and merciless satire steadfastly resist the anthropological gaze of the reader. It is a novel in whiteface. And

while black literature is almost always read as either autobiography or sociology, Schuyler's work can be read as neither.
It is one of the earliest examples of black speculative fiction.
Black No More resists the push toward preaching and the
urge toward looking backward into history. Afrofuturist before such a term existed, it insists, instead, on peering forward
into what could come to be.

My father taught me how to laugh about race. And now that
I am a parent myself, I understand what he was after in his
Schuyleresque satires. I find myself trying to transmit—
mostly unconsciously—the same lessons to my sons. I am
trying to teach them to make a mockery of the world they've
been handed—to find a way to twist it and spin it and flip it
upside down so even the most painful experiences become
material for their own private jokes. I am trying to show
them they can wear two faces. They must wear two faces.

    Black No More is funny, but it is also horrific. Humor
gives way to horror and then veers back again.

    Now is the time to read Schuyler's novel. Now more than
ever we need literature that is as fearless, observant, and ob-
stinate as *Black No More*, that speaks the uncomfortable
and unpopular truths. Now more than ever we need work
that is not afraid of its own contradictions. Through Schuyler, I am reminded—even for just the length of this short,
cutting, wild ride of a novel—of what it looks like to be free.

DANZY SENNA

Preface

Over twenty years ago a gentleman in Asbury Park, N. J. began manufacturing and advertising a preparation for the immediate and unfailing straightening of the most stubborn Negro hair. This preparation was called Kink-No-More, a name not wholly accurate since users of it were forced to renew the treatment every fortnight.

During the intervening years many chemists, professional and amateur, have been seeking the means of making the downtrodden Aframerican resemble as closely as possible his white fellow citizen. The temporarily effective preparations placed on the market have so far proved exceedingly profitable to manufacturers, advertising agencies, Negro newspapers and beauty culturists, while millions of users have registered great satisfaction at the opportunity to rid themselves of kinky hair and grow several shades lighter in color, if only for a brief time. With America's constant reiteration of the superiority of whiteness, the avid search on the part of the black masses for some key to chromatic perfection is easily understood. Now it would seem that science is on the verge of satisfying them.

Dr. Yusaburo Noguchi, head of the Noguchi Hospital in Beppu, Japan, told American newspaper reporters in October 1929, that as a result of fifteen years of painstaking research and experiment he was able to change a Negro into a white man. While he admitted that this racial metamorphosis could not be effected overnight, he maintained that

"Given time, I could change the Japanese into a race of tall blue-eyed blonds." The racial transformation, he asserted, could be brought about by glandular control and electrical nutrition.

Even more positive is the statement of Mr. Bela Cati, an electrical engineer residing in New York City, who, in a letter dated August 18, 1930, and addressed to the National Association for the Advancement of Colored People, said, in part:

> Once I myself was very strongly tanned by the sun and a European rural population thought that I was a Negro, too. I did not suffer much but the situation was disagreeable. Since that time I have studied the problem and I am convinced that the surplus of the pigment could be removed. In case you are interested and believe that with the aid of your physicians we could carry out the necessary experiments, I am willing to send you the patent specification . . . and my general terms relating to this invention. . . . The expenses are so to say negligible.

I wish to express my sincere thanks and appreciation to Mr. V. F. Calverton for his keen interest and friendly encouragement and to my wife, Josephine Schuyler, whose coöperation and criticism were of great help in completing *Black No More*.

GEORGE S. SCHUYLER

New York City,
September 1, 1930

Black No More

ONE

Max Disher stood outside the Honky Tonk Club puffing a panatela and watching the crowds of white and black folk entering the cabaret. Max was tall, dapper and smooth coffee-brown. His negroid features had a slightly satanic cast and there was an insolent nonchalance about his carriage. He wore his hat rakishly and faultless evening clothes underneath his raccoon coat. He was young, he wasn't broke, but he was damnably blue. It was New Year's Eve, 1933, but there was no spirit of gaiety and gladness in his heart. How could he share the hilarity of the crowd when he had no girl? He and Minnie, his high "yallah" flapper, had quarreled that day and everything was over between them.

"Women are mighty funny," he mused to himself, "especially yallah women. You could give them the moon and they wouldn't appreciate it." That was probably the trouble; he'd given Minnie too much. It didn't pay to spend too much on them. As soon as he'd bought her a new outfit and paid the rent on a three-room apartment, she'd grown uppity. Stuck on her color, that's what was the matter with her! He took the cigar out of his mouth and spat disgustedly.

A short, plump, cherubic black fellow, resplendent in a narrow-brimmed brown fedora, camel's hair coat and spats, strolled up and clapped him on the shoulder: "Hello, Max!" greeted the newcomer, extending a hand in a fawn-colored glove, "What's on your mind?"

"Everything, Bunny," answered the debonair Max. "That damn yallah gal o' mine's got all upstage and quit."

"Say not so!" exclaimed the short black fellow. "Why I thought you and her were all forty."

"Were, is right, kid. And after spending my dough, too! It sure makes me hot. Here I go and buy two covers at the Honky Tonk for tonight, thinkin' surely she'd come and she starts a row and quits!"

"Shucks!" exploded Bunny. "I wouldn't let that worry me none. I'd take another skirt. I wouldn't let no dame queer my New Year's."

"So would I, Wise Guy, but all the dames I know are dated up. So here I am all dressed up and no place to go."

"You got two reservations, ain't you? Well, let's you and me go in," Bunny suggested. "We may be able to break in on some party."

Max visibly brightened. "That's a good idea," he said. "You never can tell, we might run in on something good."

Swinging their canes, the two joined the throng at the entrance of the Honky Tonk Club and descended to its smoky depths. They wended their way through the maze of tables in the wake of a dancing waiter and sat down close to the dance floor. After ordering ginger ale and plenty of ice, they reared back and looked over the crowd.

Max Disher and Bunny Brown had been pals ever since the war when they soldiered together in the old 15th regiment in France. Max was one of the Aframerican Fire Insurance Company's crack agents, Bunny was a teller in the Douglass Bank and both bore the reputation of gay blades in black Harlem. The two had in common a weakness rather prevalent among Aframerican bucks: they preferred yellow women. Both swore there were three things essential to the happiness of a colored gentleman: yellow money, yellow women and yellow taxis. They had little difficulty in getting the first and none at all in getting the third but the yellow women they found flighty and fickle. It was so hard to hold them. They were so sought after that one almost required a million dollars to keep them out of the clutches of one's rivals.

"No more yallah gals for me!" Max announced with finality, sipping his drink. "I'll grab a black gal first."

"Say not so!" exclaimed Bunny, strengthening his drink from his huge silver flask. "You ain't thinkin' o' dealin' in coal, are you?"

"Well," argued his partner, "it might change my luck. You can trust a black gal; she'll stick to you."

"How do you know? You ain't never had one. Ever' gal I ever seen you with looked like an ofay."

"Humph!" grunted Max. "My next one may be an ofay, too! They're less trouble and don't ask you to give 'em the moon."

"I'm right with you, pardner," Bunny agreed, "but I gotta have one with class. None o' these Woolworth dames for me! Get you in a peck o' trouble . . . Fact is, Big Boy, ain't none o' these women no good. They all get old on the job."

They drank in silence and eyed the motley crowd around them. There were blacks, browns, yellows, and whites chatting, flirting, drinking; rubbing shoulders in the democracy of night life. A fog of tobacco smoke wreathed their heads and the din from the industrious jazz band made all but the loudest shrieks inaudible. In and out among the tables danced the waiters, trays balanced aloft, while the patrons, arrayed in colored paper caps, beat time with the orchestra, threw streamers or grew maudlin on each other's shoulders.

"Looky here! Lawdy Lawd!" exclaimed Bunny, pointing to the doorway. A party of white people had entered. They were all in evening dress and in their midst was a tall, slim, titian-haired girl who had seemingly stepped from heaven or the front cover of a magazine.

"My, my, my!" said Max, sitting up alertly.

The party consisted of two men and four women. They were escorted to a table next to the one occupied by the two colored dandies. Max and Bunny eyed them covertly. The tall girl was certainly a dream.

"Now that's my speed," whispered Bunny.

"Be yourself," said Max. "You couldn't touch her with a forty-foot pole."

"Oh, I don't know, Big Boy," Bunny beamed self-confidently, "You never can tell! You never can tell!"

"Well, I can tell," remarked Disher, "'cause she's a cracker."

"How you know that?"

"Man, I can tell a cracker a block away. I wasn't born and raised in Atlanta, Georgia, for nothin', you know. Just listen to her voice."

Bunny listened. "I believe she is," he agreed.

They kept eyeing the party to the exclusion of everything else. Max was especially fascinated. The girl was the prettiest creature he'd ever seen and he felt irresistibly drawn to her. Unconsciously he adjusted his necktie and passed his well-manicured hand over his rigidly straightened hair.

Suddenly one of the white men rose and came over to their table. They watched him suspiciously. Was he going to start something? Had he noticed that they were staring at the girl? They both stiffened at his approach.

"Say," he greeted them, leaning over the table, "do you boys know where we can get some decent liquor around here? We've run out of stuff and the waiter says he can't get any for us."

"You can get some pretty good stuff right down the street," Max informed him, somewhat relieved.

"They won't sell none to him," said Bunny. "They might think he was a Prohibition officer."

"Could one of you fellows get me some?" asked the man.

"Sure," said Max, heartily. What luck! Here was the very chance he'd been waiting for. These people might invite them over to their table. The man handed him a ten-dollar bill and Max went out bareheaded to get the liquor. In ten minutes he was back. He handed the man the quart and the change. The man gave back the change and thanked him. There was no invitation to join the party. Max returned to his table and eyed the group wistfully.

"Did he invite you in?" asked Bunny.

"I'm back here, ain't I?" answered Max, somewhat resentfully.

The floor show came on. A black-faced comedian, a corpulent shouter of mammy songs with a gin-roughened voice, three chocolate soft-shoe dancers and an octette of wriggling, practically nude, mulatto chorines.

Then midnight and pandemonium as the New Year swept in. When the din had subsided, the lights went low and the orchestra moaned the weary blues. The floor filled with couples. The two men and two of the women at the next table rose to dance. The beautiful girl and another were left behind.

"I'm going over and ask her to dance," Max suddenly announced to the surprised Bunny.

"Say not so!" exclaimed that worthy. "You're fixin' to get in dutch, Big Boy."

"Well, I'm gonna take a chance, anyhow," Max persisted, rising.

This fair beauty had hypnotized him. He felt that he would give anything for just one dance with her. Once around the floor with her slim waist in his arm would be like an eternity in heaven. Yes, one could afford to risk repulse for that.

"Don't do it, Max!" pleaded Bunny. "Them fellows are liable to start somethin'."

But Max was not to be restrained. There was no holding him back when he wanted to do a thing, especially where a comely damsel was concerned.

He sauntered over to the table in his most shiekish manner and stood looking down at the shimmering strawberry blonde. She was indeed ravishing and her exotic perfume titillated his nostrils despite the clouds of cigarette smoke.

"Would you care to dance?" he asked, after a moment's hesitation.

She looked up at him haughtily with cool green eyes, somewhat astonished at his insolence and yet perhaps secretly intrigued but her reply lacked nothing in definiteness.

"No," she said icily, "I never dance with niggers!" Then turning to her friend, she remarked: "Can you beat the nerve of these darkies?" She made a little disdainful grimace with her mouth, shrugged daintily and dismissed the unpleasant incident.

Crushed and angry, Max returned to his place without a word. Bunny laughed aloud in high glee.

"You said she was a cracker," he gurgled, "an' now I guess you know it."

"Aw, go to hell," Max grumbled.

Just then Billy Fletcher, the headwaiter, passed by. Max stopped him. "Ever see that dame in here before?" he asked.

"Been in here most every night since before Christmas," Billy replied.

"Do you know who she is?"

"Well, I heard she was some rich broad from Atlanta up here for the holidays. Why?"

"Oh, nothin'; I was just wondering."

From Atlanta! His home town. No wonder she had turned him down. Up here trying to get a thrill in the Black Belt but a thrill from observation instead of contact. Gee, but white folks were funny. They didn't want black folks' game and yet they were always frequenting Negro resorts.

At three o'clock Max and Bunny paid their check and ascended to the street. Bunny wanted to go to the breakfast dance at the Dahomey Casino but Max was in no mood for it.

"I'm going home," he announced laconically, hailing a taxi. "Good night!"

As the cab whirled up Seventh Avenue, he settled back and

thought of the girl from Atlanta. He couldn't get her out of his mind and didn't want to. At his rooming house, he paid the driver, unlocked the door, ascended to his room and undressed, mechanically. His mind was a kaleidoscope: Atlanta, sea-green eyes, slender figure, titian hair, frigid manner. "I never dance with niggers." Then he fell asleep about five o'clock and promptly dreamed of her. Dreamed of dancing with her, dining with her, motoring with her, sitting beside her on a golden throne while millions of manacled white slaves prostrated themselves before him. Then there was a nightmare of grim, gray men with shotguns, baying hounds, a heap of gasoline-soaked faggots and a screeching, fanatical mob.

He awoke covered with perspiration. His telephone was ringing and the late morning sunshine was streaming into his room. He leaped from bed and lifted the receiver.

"Say," shouted Bunny, "did you see this morning's *Times*?"

"Hell no," growled Max, "I just woke up. Why, what's in it?"

"Well, do you remember Dr. Junius Crookman, that colored fellow that went to Germany to study about three years ago? He's just come back and the *Times* claims he's announced a sure way to turn darkies white. Thought you might be interested after the way you fell for that ofay broad last night. They say Crookman's going to open a sanitarium in Harlem right away. There's your chance, Big Boy, and it's your only chance." Bunny chuckled.

"Oh, ring off," growled Max. "That's a lot of hooey."

But he was impressed and a little excited. Suppose there was something to it? He dressed hurriedly, after a cold shower, and went out to the newsstand. He bought a *Times* and scanned its columns. Yes, there it was:

NEGRO ANNOUNCES
REMARKABLE DISCOVERY
CAN CHANGE BLACK TO WHITE IN THREE DAYS.

Max went into Jimmy Johnson's restaurant and greedily read the account while awaiting his breakfast. Yes, it must be true. To think of old Crookman being able to do that! Only a few years ago he'd been just a hungry medical student around Harlem. Max put down the paper and stared vacantly out of the window. Gee, Crookman would be a millionaire in no time. He'd even be a multimillionaire. It looked as though science was to succeed where the Civil War had failed. But how could it be possible? He looked at his hands and felt at the back of his head where the straightening lotion had failed to conquer some of the knots. He toyed with his ham and eggs as he envisioned the possibilities of the discovery.

Then a sudden resolution seized him. He looked at the newspaper account again. Yes, Crookman was staying at the Phyllis Wheatley Hotel. Why not go and see what there was to this? Why not be the first Negro to try it out? Sure, it was taking a chance, but think of getting white in three days! No more jim crow. No more insults. As a white man he could go anywhere, be anything he wanted to be, do most anything he wanted to do, be a free man at last . . . and probably be able to meet the girl from Atlanta. What a vision!

He rose hurriedly, paid for his breakfast, rushed out of the door, almost ran into an aged white man carrying a sign advertising a Negro fraternity dance, and strode, almost ran, to the Phyllis Wheatley Hotel.

He tore up the steps two at a time and into the sitting room. It was crowded with white reporters from the daily newspapers and black reporters from the Negro weeklies. In their midst he recognized Dr. Junius Crookman, tall, wiry, ebony black, with a studious and polished manner. Flanking him on either side was Henry ("Hank") Johnson, the "Numbers" banker and Charlie ("Chuck") Foster, the realtor, looking very grave, important and possessive in the midst of all the hullabaloo.

"Yes," Dr. Crookman was telling the reporters while they

eagerly took down his statements, "during my first year at college I noticed a black girl on the street one day who had several irregular white patches on her face and hands. That intrigued me. I began to study up on skin diseases and found out that the girl was evidently suffering from a nervous disease known as vitiligo. It is a very rare disease. Both Negroes and Caucasians occasionally have it, but it is naturally more conspicuous on blacks than whites. It absolutely removes skin pigment and sometimes it turns a Negro completely white but only after a period of thirty or forty years. It occurred to me that if one could discover some means of artificially inducing and stimulating this nervous disease at will, one might possibly solve the American race problem. My sociology teacher had once said that there were but three ways for the Negro to solve his problem in America," he gestured with his long slender fingers, "'To either get out, get white or get along.' Since he wouldn't and couldn't get out and was getting along only differently, it seemed to me that the only thing for him was to get white." For a moment his teeth gleamed beneath his smartly waxed mustache, then he sobered and went on:

"I began to give a great deal of study to the problem during my spare time. Unfortunately there was very little information on the subject in this country. I decided to go to Germany but I didn't have the money. Just when I despaired of getting the funds to carry out my experiments and studies abroad, Mr. Johnson and Mr. Foster," he indicated the two men with a graceful wave of his hand, "came to my rescue. I naturally attribute a great deal of my success to them."

"But how is it done?" asked a reporter.

"Well," smiled Crookman, "I naturally cannot divulge the secret any more than to say that it is accomplished by electrical nutrition and glandular control. Certain gland secretions are greatly stimulated while others are considerably diminished. It is a powerful and dangerous treatment but harmless when properly done."

"How about the hair and features?" asked a Negro reporter.

"They are also changed in the process," answered the biologist. "In three days the Negro becomes to all appearances a Caucasian."

"But is the transformation transferred to the offspring?" persisted the Negro newspaperman.

"As yet," replied Crookman, "I have discovered no way to accomplish anything so revolutionary but I am able to transform a black infant to a white one in twenty-four hours."

"Have you tried it on any Negroes yet?" queried a skeptical white journalist.

"Why of course I have," said the Doctor, slightly nettled. "I would not have made my announcement if I had not done so. Come here, Sandol," he called, turning to a pale white youth standing on the outskirts of the crowd, who was the most Nordic-looking person in the room. "This man is a Senegalese, a former aviator in the French Army. He is living proof that what I claim is true."

Dr. Crookman then displayed a photograph of a very black man, somewhat resembling Sandol but with bushy Negro hair, flat nose and full lips. "This," he announced proudly, "is Sandol as he looked before taking my treatment. What I have done to him I can do to any Negro. He is in good physical and mental condition as you all can see."

The assemblage was properly awed. After taking a few more notes and a number of photographs of Dr. Crookman, his associates and of Sandol, the newspapermen retired. Only the dapper Max Disher remained.

"Hello, Doc!" he said, coming forward and extending his hand. "Don't you remember me? I'm Max Disher."

"Why certainly I remember you, Max," replied the biologist, rising cordially. "Been a long time since we've seen each other but you're looking as sharp as ever. How's things?"

The two men shook hands.

"Oh, pretty good. Say, Doc, how's chances to get you to try that thing on me? You must be looking for volunteers."

"Yes, I am, but not just yet. I've got to get my equipment set up first. I think now I'll be ready for business in a couple of weeks."

Henry Johnson, the beefy, sleek-jowled, mulatto "Numbers" banker, chuckled and nudged Dr. Crookman. "Old Max ain't losin' no time, Doc. When that niggah gits white Ah bet he'll make up fo' los' time with these ofay girls."

Charlie Foster, small, slender, grave, amber-colored, and laconic, finally spoke up: "Seems all right, Junius, but there'll be hell to pay when you whiten up a lot o' these darkies and them mulatto babies start appearing here and there. Watcha gonna do then?"

"Oh, quit singin' th' blues, Chuck," boomed Johnson. "Don't cross bridges 'til yuh come tuh 'em. Doc'll fix that okeh. Besides, we'll have mo' money'n Henry Ford by that time."

"There'll be no difficulties whatever," assured Crookman rather impatiently.

"Let's hope not."

Next day the newspaper carried a long account of the interview with Dr. Junius Crookman interspersed with photographs of him, his backers and of the Senegalese who had been turned white. It was the talk of the town and was soon the talk of the country. Long editorials were written about the discovery, learned societies besieged the Negro biologist with offers of lecture engagements, magazines begged him for articles, but he turned down all offers and refused to explain his treatment. This attitude was decried as unbecoming a scientist and it was insinuated and even openly stated that nothing more could be expected from a Negro.

But Crookman ignored the clamor of the public, and with the financial help of his associates planned the great and lucrative experiment of turning Negroes into Caucasians.

The impatient Max Disher saw him as often as possible and kept track of developments. He yearned to be the first treated and didn't want to be caught napping. Two objects were uppermost in his mind: To get white and to Atlanta. The statuesque and haughty blonde was ever in his thoughts. He was head over heels in love with her and realized there was no hope for him to ever win her as long as he was brown. Each day he would walk past the tall building that was to be the Crookman Sanitarium, watching the workmen and delivery trucks; wondering how much longer he would have to wait before entering upon the great adventure.

At last the sanitarium was ready for business. Huge advertisements appeared in the local Negro weeklies. Black Harlem was on its toes. Curious throngs of Negroes and whites stood in front of the austere six-story building gazing up at its windows.

Inside, Crookman, Johnson and Foster stood nervously about while hustling attendants got everything in readiness. Outside they could hear the murmur of the crowd.

"That means money, Chuck," boomed Johnson, rubbing his beefsteak hands together.

"Yeh," replied the realtor, "but there's one more thing I wanna get straight: How about that darky dialect? You can't change that."

"It isn't necessary, my dear Foster," explained the physician, patiently. "There is no such thing as Negro dialect, except in literature and drama. It is a well-known fact among informed persons that a Negro from a given section speaks the same dialect as his white neighbors. In the South you can't tell over the telephone whether you are talking to a white man or a Negro. The same is true in New York when a Northern Negro speaks into the receiver. I have noticed the same thing in the hills of West Virginia and Tennessee. The educated Haitian speaks the purest French and the Jamaican Negro sounds exactly like an Englishman. There are no racial or color dialects; only sectional dialects."

"Guess you're right," agreed Foster, grudgingly.

"I know I'm right. Moreover, even if my treatment did not change the so-called Negro lips, even that would prove to be no obstacle."

"How come, Doc," asked Johnson.

"Well, there are plenty of Caucasians who have lips quite as thick and noses quite as broad as any of us. As a matter of fact there has been considerable exaggeration about the contrast between Caucasian and Negro features. The cartoonists and minstrel men have been responsible for it very largely. Some Negroes like the Somalis, Filanis, Egyptians, Hausas and Abyssinians have very thin lips and nostrils. So also have the Malagasys of Madagascar. Only in certain small sections of Africa do the Negroes possess extremely pendulous lips and very broad nostrils. On the other hand, many so-called Caucasians, particularly the Latins, Jews and South Irish, and frequently the most Nordic of peoples like the Swedes, show almost Negroid lips and noses. Black up some white folks and they could deceive a resident of Benin. Then when you consider that less than twenty per cent of our Negroes are without Caucasian ancestry and that close to thirty per cent have American Indian ancestry, it is readily seen that there cannot be the wide difference in Caucasian and Afro-American facial characteristics that most people imagine."

"Doc, you sho' knows yo' onions," said Johnson, admiringly. "Doan pay no 'tenshun to that ole Doubtin' Thomas. He'd holler starvation in a pie shop."

There was a commotion outside and an angry voice was heard above the hum of low conversation. Then Max Disher burst in the door with a guard hanging onto his coat tail.

"Let loose o' me, Boy," he quarreled. "I got an engagement here. Doc, tell this man something, will you?"

Crookman nodded to the guard to release the insurance man. "Well, I see you're right on time, Max."

"I told you I'd be Johnny-on-the-spot, didn't I?" said Disher, inspecting his clothes to see if they had been wrinkled.

"Well, if you're all ready, go into the receiving room there, sign the register and get into one of those bathrobes. You're first on the list."

The three partners looked at each other and grinned as Max disappeared into a small room at the end of the corridor. Dr. Crookman went into his office to don his white trousers, shoes and smock; Johnson and Foster entered the business office to supervise the clerical staff, while white-coated figures darted back and forth through the corridors. Outside, the murmuring of the vast throng grew more audible.

Johnson showed all of his many gold teeth in a wide grin as he glanced out the window and saw the queue of Negroes already extending around the corner. "Man, man, man!" he chuckled to Foster, "at fifty dollars a th'ow this thing's gonna have th' numbah business beat all hollow."

"Hope so," said Foster, gravely.

Max Disher, arrayed only in a hospital bathrobe and a pair of slippers, was escorted to the elevator by two white-coated attendants. They got off on the sixth floor and walked to the end of the corridor. Max was trembling with excitement and anxiety. Suppose something should go wrong? Suppose Doc should make a mistake? He thought of the Elks' excursion every summer to Bear Mountain, the high yellow Minnie and her colorful apartment, the pleasant evenings at the Da-homey Casino doing the latest dances with the brown belles of Harlem, the prancing choruses at the Lafayette Theater, the hours he had whiled away at Boogie's and the Honky Tonk Club, and he hesitated. Then he envisioned his future as a white man, probably as the husband of the tall blonde from Atlanta, and with firm resolve, he entered the door of the mysterious chamber.

He quailed as he saw the formidable apparatus of sparkling nickel. It resembled a cross between a dentist's chair and an electric chair. Wires and straps, bars and levers protruded from it and a great nickel headpiece, like the helmet of a knight, hung over it. The room had only a skylight and no sound entered it from the outside. Around the walls were cases of instruments and shelves of bottles filled with strangely colored fluids. He gasped with fright and would have made for the door but the two husky attendants held him firmly, stripped off his robe and bound him in the chair. There was no retreat. It was either the beginning or the end.

TWO

Slowly, haltingly, Max Disher dragged his way down the hall to the elevator, supported on either side by an attendant. He felt terribly weak, emptied and nauseated; his skin twitched and was dry and feverish; his insides felt very hot and sore. As the trio walked slowly along the corridor, a blue-green light would ever and anon blaze through one of the doorways as a patient was taken in. There was a low hum and throb of machinery and an acid odor filled the air. Uniformed nurses and attendants hurried back and forth at their tasks. Everything was quiet, swift, efficient, sinister.

He felt so thankful that he had survived the ordeal of that horrible machine so akin to the electric chair. A shudder passed over him at the memory of the hours he had passed in its grip, fed at intervals with revolting concoctions. But when they reached the elevator and he saw himself in the mirror, he was startled, overjoyed. White at last! Gone was the smooth brown complexion. Gone were the slightly full lips and Ethiopian nose. Gone was the nappy hair that he had straightened so meticulously ever since the kink-no-more lotions first wrenched Aframericans from the tyranny and torture of the comb. There would be no more expenditures for skin whiteners; no more discrimination; no more obstacles in his path. He was free! The world was his oyster and he had the open sesame of a pork-colored skin!

The reflection in the mirror gave him new life and strength. He now stood erect, without support, and grinned at the two tall, black attendants. "Well, Boys," he crowed, "I'm all set now. That machine of Doc's worked like a charm. Soon's I get a feed under my belt I'll be okeh."

Six hours later, bathed, fed, clean-shaven, spry, blond and jubilant, he emerged from the outpatient ward and tripped gaily down the corridor to the main entrance. He was through with coons, he resolved, from now on. He glanced in a superior manner at the long line of black and brown folk on one side of the corridor, patiently awaiting treatment. He saw many persons whom he knew but none of them recognized him. It thrilled him to feel that he was now indistinguishable from nine-tenths of the people of the United States; one of the great majority. Ah, it was good not to be a Negro any longer!

As he sought to open the front door, the strong arm of a guard restrained him. "Wait a minute," the man said, "and we'll help you get through the mob."

A moment or two later Max found himself the center of a flying wedge of five or six husky special policemen, cleaving through a milling crowd of colored folk. From the top step of the sanitarium he had noticed the crowd spread over the sidewalk, into the street and around the corners. Fifty traffic policemen strained and sweated to keep prospective patients in line and out from under the wheels of taxicabs and trucks.

Finally he reached the curb, exhausted from the jostling and squeezing, only to be set upon by a mob of newspaper photographers and reporters. As the first person to take the treatment, he was naturally the center of attraction for about fifteen of these journalistic gnats. They asked a thousand questions seemingly all at once. What was his name? How did he feel? What was he going to do? Would he marry a white woman? Did he intend to continue living in Harlem?

Max would say nothing. In the first place, he thought to himself, if they're so anxious to know all this stuff, they ought to be willing to pay for it. He needed money if he was going to be able to thoroughly enjoy being white; why not get some by selling his story? The reporters, male and female, begged him almost with tears in their eyes for a statement but he was adamant.

While they were wrangling, an empty taxicab drove up. Pushing the inquisitive reporters to one side, Max leaped into it and yelled "Central Park!" It was the only place he could think of at the moment. He wanted to have time to compose his mind, to plan the future in this great world of whiteness. As the cab lurched forward, he turned and was astonished to find another occupant, a pretty girl.

"Don't be scared," she smiled. "I knew you would want to get away from that mob so I went around the corner and got a cab for you. Come along with me and I'll get everything fixed up for you. I'm a reporter from *The Scimitar*. We'll give you a lot of money for your story." She talked rapidly. Max's first impulse had been to jump out of the cab, even at the risk of having to face again the mob of reporters and photographers he had sought to escape, but he changed his mind when he heard mention of money.

"How much?" he asked, eyeing her. She was very comely and he noted that her ankles were well turned.

"Oh, probably a thousand dollars," she replied.

"Well, that sounds good." A thousand dollars! What a time he could have with that! Broadway for him as soon as he got paid off.

As they sped down Seventh Avenue, the newsboys were yelling the latest editions. "Ex—try! Ex—try! Blacks turning white! Blacks turning white! . . . Read all about the gr-r-reat dis—covery! Paper, Mister! Paper! . . . Read all about Dr. Crookman."

He settled back while they drove through the park and glanced frequently at the girl by his side. She looked mighty good; wonder could he talk business with her? Might go to dinner and a cabaret. That would be the best way to start.

"What did you say your name was?" he began.

"I didn't say," she stalled.

"Well, you have a name, haven't you?" he persisted.

"Suppose I have?"

"You're not scared to tell it, are you?"

"Why do you want to know my name?"

"Well, there's nothing wrong about wanting to know a pretty girl's name, is there?"

"Well, my name's Smith, Sybil Smith. Now are you satisfied?"

"Not yet. I want to know something more. How would you like to go to dinner with me tonight?"

"I don't know and I won't know until I've had the experience." She smiled coquettishly. Going out with him, she figured, would make the basis of a rattling good story for tomorrow's paper. "Negro's first night as a Caucasian!" Fine!

"Say, you're a regular fellow," he said, beaming upon her. "I'll get a great kick out of going to dinner with you because you'll be the only one in the place that'll know I'm a Negro."

Down at the office of *The Scimitar*, it didn't take Max long to come to an agreement, tell his story to a stenographer and get a sheaf of crisp, new bills. As he left the building a couple of hours later with Miss Smith on his arm, the newsboys were already crying the extra edition carrying the first installment of his strange tale. A huge photograph of him occupied the entire front page of the tabloid. Lucky for him that he'd given his name as William Small, he thought.

He was annoyed and a little angered. What did they want to put his picture all over the front of the paper for? Now everybody would know who he was. He had undergone the tortures of Doc Crookman's devilish machine in order to escape the conspicuousness of a dark skin and now he was being made conspicuous because he had once had a dark skin! Could one never escape the plagued race problem?

"Don't worry about that," comforted Miss Smith. "Nobody'll recognize you. There are thousands of white people, yes millions, that look like you do." She took his arm and snuggled up closer. She wanted to make him feel at home. It wasn't often a poor, struggling newspaper woman got a chap with a big bankroll to take her out for the evening. Moreover, the description she would write of the experience might win her a promotion.

They walked down Broadway in the blaze of white lights to a dinner-dance place. To Max it was like being in heaven. He had strolled through the Times Square district before but never with such a feeling of absolute freedom and sureness. No one now looked at him curiously because he was with a white girl, as they had when he came down there with Minnie, his former octoroon lady friend. Gee, it was great!

They dined and they danced. Then they went to a cabaret, where, amid smoke, noise and body smells, they drank what was purported to be whiskey and watched a semi-nude chorus do its stuff. Despite his happiness Max found it pretty dull. There was something lacking in these ofay places of amusement or else there was something present that one didn't find in the black-and-tan resorts in Harlem. The joy and abandon here was obviously forced. Patrons went to extremes to show each other they were having a wonderful time. It was all so strained and quite unlike anything to which he had been accustomed. The Negroes, it seemed to him, were much gayer, enjoyed themselves more deeply and yet they were more restrained, actually more refined. Even their dancing was different. They followed the rhythm accurately, effortlessly and with easy grace; these lumbering couples, out of step half the time and working as strenuously as stevedores emptying the bowels of a freighter, were noisy, awkward, inelegant. At their best they were gymnastic where the Negroes were sensuous. He felt a momentary pang of mingled disgust, disillusionment and nostalgia. But it was only momentary. He looked across at the comely Sybil and then around at the other white women, many of whom were very pretty and expensively gowned, and the sight temporarily drove from his mind the thoughts that had been occupying him.

They parted at three o'clock, after she had given him her telephone number. She pecked him lightly on the cheek in payment, doubtless, for a pleasant evening's entertainment. Somewhat disappointed because she had failed to show any interest in his expressed curiosity about the interior of her apartment, he directed the chauffeur to drive him to Harlem. After all, he argued to himself in defense of his action, he had to get his things.

As the cab turned out of Central Park at 110th Street he felt, curiously enough, a feeling of peace. There were all the old familiar sights: the all-night speakeasies, the frankfurter stands, the loiterers, the late pedestrians, the chop suey joints, the careening taxicabs, the bawdy laughter.

He couldn't resist the temptation to get out at 133rd Street and go down to Boogie's place, the hangout of his gang. He tapped, an eye peered through a hole, appraised him critically, then disappeared and the hole was closed. There was silence.

Max frowned. What was the matter with old Bob? Why didn't he open that door? The cold January breeze swept down into the little court where he stood and made him shiver. He knocked a little louder, more insistently. The eye appeared again.

"Who's 'at?" growled the doorkeeper.

"It's me, Max Disher," replied the ex-Negro.

"Go 'way f'm here, white man. Dis heah place is closed."

"Is Bunny Brown in there?" asked Max in desperation.

"Yeh, he's heah. Does yuh know him? Well, Ah'll call 'im out heah and see if he knows you."

Max waited in the cold for about two or three minutes and then the door suddenly opened and Bunny Brown, a little unsteady, came out. He peered at Max in the light from the electric bulb over the door.

"Hello, Bunny," Max greeted him. "Don't know me, do you? It's me, Max Disher. You recognize my voice, don't you?"

Bunny looked again, rubbed his eyes and shook his head. Yes, the voice was Max Disher's, but this man was white. Still, when he smiled his eyes revealed the same sardonic twinkle—so characteristic of his friend.

"Max," he blurted out, "is that you, sure enough? Well, for cryin' out loud! Damned 'f you ain't been up there to Crookman's and got fixed up. Well, hush my mouth! Bob, open that door. This is old Max Disher. Done gone up there to Crookman's and got all white on my hands. He's just too tight, with his blond hair, 'n everything."

Bob opened the door, the two friends entered, sat down at one of the small round tables in the narrow, smoke-filled cellar and were soon surrounded with cronies. They gazed raptly at his colorless skin, commented on the veins showing blue through the epidermis, stroked his ash-blond hair and listened with mouths open to his remarkable story.

"Watcha gonna do now, Max?" asked Boogie, the rangy, black, bullet-headed proprietor.

"I know just what that joker's gonna do," said Bunny. "He's goin' back to Atlanta. Am I right, Big Boy?"

"You ain't wrong," Max agreed. "I'm goin' right on down there, brother, and make up for lost time."

"Whadayah mean?" asked Boogie.

"Boy, it would take me until tomorrow night to tell you and then you wouldn't understand."

The two friends strolled up the avenue. Both were rather mum. They had been inseparable pals since the stirring days in France. Now they were about to be parted. It wasn't as if Max was going across the ocean to some foreign country; there would be a wider gulf separating them: the great sea of color. They both thought about it.

"I'll be pretty lonesome without you, Bunny."

"It ain't you, Big Boy."

"Well, why don't you go ahead and get white and then we could stay together. I'll give you the money."

"Say not so! Where'd you get so much jack all of a sudden?" asked Bunny.

"Sold my story to *The Scimitar* for a grand."

"Paid in full?"

"Wasn't paid in part!"

"All right, then, I'll take you up, Heavy Sugar." Bunny held out his plump hand and Max handed him a hundred-dollar bill.

They were near the Crookman Sanitarium. Although it was five o'clock on a Sunday morning, the building was brightly lighted from cellar to roof and the hum of electric motors could be heard, low and powerful. A large electric sign hung from the roof to the second floor. It represented a huge arrow outlined in green with the words BLACK-NO-MORE running its full length vertically. A black face was depicted at the lower end of the arrow while at the top shone a white face to which the arrow was pointed. First would appear the outline of the arrow; then, BLACK-NO-MORE would flash on and off. Following that the black face would appear at the bottom and beginning at the lower end the long arrow with its lettering would appear progressively until its tip was reached, when the white face at the top would blazon forth. After that the sign would flash off and on and the process would be repeated.

In front of the sanitarium milled a half-frozen crowd of close to four thousand Negroes. A riot squad armed with rifles, machine guns and tear gas bombs maintained some semblance of order. A steel cable stretched from lamp post to lamp post the entire length of the block kept the struggling mass of humanity on the sidewalk and out of the path of the traffic. It seemed as if all Harlem were there. As the two friends reached the outskirts of the mob, an ambulance from the Harlem Hospital drove up and carried away two women who had been trampled upon.

Lined up from the door to the curb was a gang of tough special guards dredged out of the slums. Grim Irish from Hell's Kitchen, rough Negroes from around 133rd Street and 5th Avenue (New York's "Beale Street") and tough Italians from the lower West Side. They managed with difficulty to keep an aisle cleared for incoming and outgoing patients. Near the curb were stationed the reporters and photographers.

The noise rose and fell. First there would be a low hum of voices. Steadily it would rise and rise in increasing volume as the speakers became more animated and reach its climax in a great animal-like roar as the big front door would open and a whitened Negro would emerge. Then the mass would surge forward to peer at and question the ersatz Nordic. Sometimes the ex-Ethiopian would quail before the mob and jump back into the building. Then the hardboiled guards would form a flying squad and hustle him to a waiting taxicab. Other erstwhile Aframericans issuing from the building would grin broadly, shake hands with friends and relatives and start to graphically describe their experience while the Negroes around them enviously admired their clear white skins.

In between these appearances the hot dog and peanut vendors did a brisk trade, along with the numerous pickpockets of the district. One slender, anemic, ratty-looking mulatto Negro was almost beaten to death by a gigantic black laundress whose purse he had snatched. A Negro selling hot roasted sweet potatoes did a land-office business while the neighboring saloons, that had increased so rapidly in number since the enactment of the Volstead Law that many of their Italian proprietors paid substantial income taxes, sold scores of gallons of incredibly atrocious hootch.

"Well, bye, bye, Max," said Bunny, extending his hand. "I'm goin' in an' try my luck."

"So long, Bunny. See you in Atlanta. Write me general delivery."

"Why, ain't you gonna wait for me, Max?"

"Naw! I'm fed up on this town."

"Oh, you ain't kiddin' me, Big Boy. I know you want to look up that broad you saw in the Honky Tonk New Year's Eve," Bunny beamed.

Max grinned and blushed slightly. They shook hands and parted. Bunny ran up the aisle from the curb, opened the sanitarium door and without turning around, disappeared within.

For a minute or so, Max stood irresolutely in the midst of the gibbering crowd of people. Unaccountably he felt at home here among these black folk. Their jests, scraps of conversation and lusty laughter all seemed like heavenly music. Momentarily he felt a disposition to stay among them, to share again their troubles which they seemed always to bear with a lightness that was yet not indifference. But then, he suddenly realized with just a tiny trace of remorse that the past was forever gone. He must seek other pastures, other pursuits, other playmates, other loves. He was white now. Even if he wished to stay among his folk, they would be either jealous or suspicious of him, as they were of most octoroons and nearly all whites. There was no other alternative than to seek his future among the Caucasians with whom he now rightfully belonged.

And after all, he thought, it was a glorious new adventure. His eyes twinkled and his pulse quickened as he thought of it. Now he could go anywhere, associate with anybody, be anything he wanted to be. He suddenly thought of the comely miss he had seen in the Honky Tonk on New Year's Eve and the greatly enlarged field from which he could select his loves. Yes, indeed there were advantages in being white. He brightened and viewed the tightly-packed black folk around him with a superior air. Then, thinking again of his clothes at Mrs. Blandish's, the money in his pocket and the prospect for the first time of riding into Atlanta in a Pullman car and not as a Pullman porter, he turned and pushed his way through the throng.

He strolled up West 139th Street to his rooming place, stepping lightly and sniffing the early morning air. How good it was to be free, white and to possess a bankroll! He fumbled in his pocket for his little mirror and looked at himself again and again from several angles. He stroked his pale blond hair and secretly congratulated himself that he would no longer need to straighten it nor be afraid to wet it. He gazed raptly at his smooth, white hands with the blue veins showing through. What a miracle Dr. Crookman had wrought!

As he entered the hallway, the mountainous form of his landlady loomed up. She jumped back as she saw his face.

"What you doing in here?" she almost shouted. "Where'd you get a key to this house?"

"It's me, Max Disher," he assured her with a grin at her astonishment. "Don't know me, do you?"

She gazed incredulously into his face. "Is that you sure enough, Max? How in the devil did you get so white?"

He explained and showed her a copy of *The Scimitar* containing his story. She switched on the hall light and read it. Contrasting emotions played over her face, for Mrs. Blandish was known in the business world as Mme. Sisseretta Blandish, the beauty specialist, who owned the swellest hair-straightening parlor in Harlem. Business, she thought to herself, was bad enough, what with all of the competition, without this Dr. Crookman coming along and killing it altogether.

"Well," she sighed, "I suppose you're going downtown to live, now. I always said niggers didn't really have any race pride."

Uneasy, Max made no reply. The fat, brown woman turned with a disdainful sniff and disappeared into a room at the end of the hall. He ran lightly upstairs to pack his things.

An hour later, as the taxicab bearing him and his luggage

bowled through Central Park, he was in high spirits. He would go down to the Pennsylvania Station and get a Pullman straight into Atlanta. He would stop there at the best hotel. He wouldn't hunt up any of his folks. No, that would be too dangerous. He would just play around, enjoy life and laugh at the white folks up his sleeve. God! What an adventure! What a treat it would be to mingle with white people in places where as a youth he had never dared to enter. At last he felt like an American citizen. He flecked the ash of his panatela out of the open window of the cab and sank back in the seat feeling at peace with the world.

THREE

Dr. Junius Crookman, looking tired and worn, poured himself another cup of coffee from the percolator nearby and, turning to Hank Johnson, asked "What about that new electrical apparatus?"

"On th' way, Doc. On th' way," replied the former Numbers baron. "Just talkin' to th' man this mornin'. He says we'll get it tomorrow, maybe."

"Well, we certainly need it," said Chuck Foster, who sat beside him on the large leather divan. "We can't handle all of the business as it is."

"How about those new places you're buying?" asked the physician.

"Well, I've bought the big private house on Edgecombe Avenue for fifteen thousand and the workmen are getting it in shape now. It ought to be ready in about a week if nothing happens," Foster informed him.

"If nuthin' happens?" echoed Johnson. "Whut's gonna happen? We're settin' on th' world, ain't we? Our racket's within th' law, ain't it? We're makin' money faster'n we can take it in, ain't we? Whut could happen? This here is the best and safest graft I've ever been in."

"Oh, you never can tell," cautioned the quondam realtor. "These white newspapers, especially in the South, are beginning to write some pretty strong editorials against us and we've only been running two weeks. You know how easy it is to stir up the fanatical element. Before we know it they're liable to get a law passed against us."

"Not if I c'n git to th' legislature first," interrupted Johnson. "Yuh know, Ah knows how tuh handle these white folks. If yuh 'Say it with Bucks' you c'n git anything yuh want."

"There is something in what Foster says, though," Dr. Crookman said. "Just look at this bunch of clippings we got in this morning. Listen to these: 'The Viper in Our Midst,' from the Richmond *Blade;* 'The Menace of Science' from the Memphis *Bugle;* 'A Challenge to Every White Man' from the Dallas *Sun;* 'Police Battle Black Mob Seeking White Skins,' from the Atlanta *Topic;* 'Negro Doctor Admits Being Taught by Germans,' from the St. Louis *North American.* Here's a line or two from an editorial in the *Oklahoma City Hatchet:* 'There are times when the welfare of our race must take precedence over law. Opposed as we always have been to mob violence as the worst enemy of democratic government, we cannot help but feel that the intelligent white men and women of New York City who are interested in the purity and preservation of their race should not permit the challenge of Crookmanism to go unanswered, even though these black scoundrels may be within the law. There are too many criminals in this country already hiding behind the skirts of the law.'

"And lastly, one from the Tallahassee *Announcer* says: 'While it is the right of every citizen to do what he wants to do with his money, the white people of the United States cannot remain indifferent to this discovery and its horrible potentialities. Hundreds of Negroes with newly-acquired white skins have already entered white society and thousands will follow them. The black race from one end of the country to the other has in two short weeks gone completely crazy over the prospect of getting white. Day by day we see the color line which we have so laboriously established being rapidly destroyed. There would not be so much cause for alarm in this, were it not for the fact that this vitiligo is not hereditary. In other words, THE OFFSPRING OF THESE WHITENED NEGROES WILL BE NEGROES! This means that your daughter, having married a supposed white man, may find herself with a black baby! Will the proud white men of the Southland so far forget their traditions as to remain idle while this devilish work is going on?'"

"No use singin' th' blues," counseled Johnson. "We ain' gonna be both'ed heah, even if them crackahs down South do raise a little hell. Jus' listen to th' sweet music of that mob out theah! Eve'y scream means fifty bucks. On'y reason we ain't makin' mo' money is' cause we ain't got no mo' room."

"That's right," Dr. Crookman agreed. "We've turned out one hundred a day for fourteen days." He leaned back and lit a cigarette.

"At fifty bucks a th'ow," interrupted Johnson, "that means we've took in seventy thousand dollahs. Great Day in th' mornin'! Didn't know tha was so much jack in Harlem."

"Yes," continued Crookman, "we're taking in thirty-five thousand dollars a week. As soon as you and Foster get that other place fixed up we'll be making twice that much."

From the hallway came the voice of the switchboard operator monotonously droning out her instructions: "No, Dr. Crookman cannot see anyone. . . . Dr. Crookman has nothing to say. . . . Dr. Crookman will issue a statement shortly. . . . Fifty dollars. . . . No, Dr. Crookman isn't a mulatto. . . . I'm very sorry but I cannot answer that question."

The three friends sat in silence amid the hum of activity around them. Hank Johnson smiled down at the end of his cigar as he thought back over his rather colorful and hectic career. To think that today he was one of the leading Negroes of the world, one who was taking an active and important part in solving the most vexatious problem in American life, and yet only ten years before he had been working on a Carolina chain gang. Two years he had toiled on the roads under the hard eye and ready rifle of a cruel white guard; two years

of being beaten, kicked and cursed, of poor food and vermin-
infested habitations; two years for participating in a little
crap game. Then he had drifted to Charleston, got a job in
a pool room, had a stroke of luck with the dice, come to New
York and landed right in the midst of the Numbers racket.
Becoming a collector or "runner," he had managed his affairs well enough to be able to start out soon as a "banker."
Money had poured in from Negroes eager to chance one cent
in the hope of winning six dollars. Some won but most lost
and he had prospered. He had purchased an apartment
house, paid off the police, dabbled in the bail bond game,
given a couple of thousand dollars to advance Negro Art and
been elected Grand Permanent Shogun of the Ancient and
Honorable Order of Crocodiles, Harlem's largest and most
prosperous secret society. Then young Crookman had come
to him with his proposition. At first he had hesitated about
helping him but later was persuaded to do so when the young
man bitterly complained that the dirty Negroes would not
help to pay for the studies abroad. What a stroke of luck,
getting in on the ground floor like this! They'd all be richer
than Rockefeller inside of a year. Twelve million Negroes at
fifty dollars apiece! Great Day in the morning! Hank spat
regally into the brass cuspidor across the office and reared
back contentedly on the soft cushion of the divan.

Chuck Foster was also seeing his career in retrospect. His
life had not been as colorful as that of Hank Johnson. The
son of a Birmingham barber, he had enjoyed such educational
advantages as that community afforded the darker brethren;
had become a schoolteacher, an insurance agent and a social
worker in turn. Then, along with the tide of migration, he
had drifted first to Cincinnati, then to Pittsburgh and finally
to New York. There the real estate field, unusually lucrative
because of the paucity of apartments for the increasing Negro
population, had claimed him. Cautious, careful, thrifty and
devoid of sentimentality, he had prospered, but not without
some ugly rumors being broadcast about his sharp business

methods. As he slowly worked his way up to the top of Harlem society, he had sought to live down this reputation for double-dealing and shifty practices, all too true of the bulk of his fellow realtors in the district, by giving large sums to the Young Men's and Young Women's Christian Associations, by offering scholarships to young Negroes, by staging elaborate parties to which the dicty Negroes of the community were invited. He had been glad of the opportunity to help subsidize young Crookman's studies abroad when Hank Johnson pointed out the possibilities of the venture. Now, although the results so far exceeded his wildest dreams, his natural conservatism and timidity made him somewhat pessimistic about the future. He supposed a hundred dire results of their activities and only the day before he had increased the amount of his life insurance. His mind was filled with doubts. He didn't like so much publicity. He wanted a sort of genteel popularity but no notoriety.

Despite the coffee and cigarettes, Dr. Junius Crookman was sleepy. The responsibility, the necessity of overseeing the work of his physicians and nurses, the insistence of the newspapers and the medical profession that he reveal the secrets of his treatment and a thousand other vexatious details had kept him from getting proper rest. He had, indeed, spent most of his time in the sanitarium.

This hectic activity was new to him. Up until a month ago his thirty-five years had been peaceful and, in the main, studious ones. The son of an Episcopal clergyman, he had been born and raised in a city in central New York, his associates carefully selected in order to protect him as much as possible from the defeatist psychology so prevalent among American Negroes and given every opportunity and inducement to learn his profession and become a thoroughly cultivated and civilized man. His parents, though poor, were proud and boasted that they belonged to the Negro aristocracy. He had had to work his way through college because of the failure of his father's health but he had come very little in contact with the crudity, coarseness and cruelty of life. He had been monotonously successful but he was sensible enough to believe that a large part of it was due, like most success, to chance. He saw in his great discovery the solution to the most annoying problem in American life. Obviously, he reasoned, if there were no Negroes, there could be no Negro problem. Without a Negro problem, Americans could concentrate their attention on something constructive. Through his efforts and the activities of Black-No-More, Incorporated, it would be possible to do what agitation, education and legislation had failed to do. He was naïvely surprised that there should be opposition to his work. Like most men with a vision, a plan, a program or a remedy, he fondly imagined people to be intelligent enough to accept a good thing when it was offered to them, which was conclusive evidence that he knew little about the human race.

Dr. Crookman prided himself above all on being a great lover of his race. He had studied its history, read of its struggles and kept up with its achievements. He subscribed to six or seven Negro weekly newspapers and two of the magazines. He was so interested in the continued progress of the American Negroes that he wanted to remove all obstacles in their path by depriving them of their racial characteristics. His home and office were filled with African masks and paintings of Negroes by Negroes. He was what was known in Negro society as a Race Man. He was wedded to everything black except the black woman—his wife was a white girl with remote Negro ancestry, of the type that Negroes were wont to describe as being "able to pass for white." While abroad he had spent his spare time ransacking the libraries for facts about the achievements of Negroes and having liaisons with comely and available fraus and frauliens.

"Well, Doc," said Hank Johnson, suddenly, "you'd bettah go on home 'n git some sleep. Ain' no use killin' you'sef. Eve'thing's gonna be all right heah. You ain' gotta thing tuh worry 'bout."

"How's he gonna get out of here with that mob in front?" Chuck inquired. "A man almost needs a tank to get through that crowd of darkies."

"Oh, Ah've got all that fixed, Calamity Jane," Johnson remarked casually. "All he's gotta do is tuh go on down stahs tuh the basem'nt, go out th' back way an' step into th' alley. My car'll be theah waitin' fo' 'im."

"That's awfully nice of you, Johnson," said the physician. "I am dead tired. I think I'll be a new man if I can get a few hours of sleep."

A black man in white uniform opened the door and announced: "Mrs. Crookman!" He held the door open for the Doctor's petite, stylishly dressed wife to enter. The three men sprang to their feet. Johnson and Foster eyed the beautiful little octoroon appreciatively as they bowed, thinking how easily she could "pass for white," which would have been something akin to a piece of anthracite coal passing for black.

"Darling!" she exclaimed, turning to her husband. "Why don't you come home and get some rest? You'll be ill if you keep on in this way."

"Jus' whut Ah bin tellin' him, Mrs. Crookman," Johnson hastened to say. "We got eve'ything fixed tuh send 'im off."

"Well, then, Junius, we'd better be going," she said decisively.

Putting on a long overcoat over his white uniform, Dr. Crookman wearily and meekly followed his spouse out of the door.

"Mighty nice-looking girl, Mrs. Crookman," Foster observed.

"Nice-lookin'!" echoed Johnson, with mock amazement. "Why, nigguh, that ooman would make uh rabbit hug uh houn'. Doc sez she's culled, an' she sez so, but she looks mighty white tuh me."

"Everything that looks white ain't white in this man's country," Foster replied.

Meantime there was feverish activity in Harlem's financial institutions. At the Douglass Bank the tellers were busier than bootleggers on Christmas Eve. Moreover, they were short-handed because of the mysterious absence of Bunny Brown. A long queue of Negroes extended down one side of the bank, out of the front door and around the corner, while bank attendants struggled to keep them in line. Everybody was drawing out money; no one was depositing. In vain the bank officials pleaded with them not to withdraw their funds. The Negroes were adamant: they wanted their money and wanted it quick. Day after day this had gone on ever since Black-No-More, Incorporated, had started turning Negroes white. At first, efforts were made to bulldoze and intimidate the depositors but that didn't succeed. These people were in no mood to be trifled with. A lifetime of being Negroes in the United States had convinced them that there was great advantage in being white.

"Mon, whutcha tahlk ab't?" scoffed a big, black British West Indian woman with whom an official was remonstrating not to draw out her money. "Dis heah's mah mahney, ain't it? Yuh use mah mahney all time, aintcha? Whutcha mean, Ah shouldn't draw't out? . . . You gimme mah mahney or Ah broke up dis place!"

"Are you closing your account, Mr. Robinson?" a soft-voiced mulatto teller inquired of a big, rusty stevedore.

"Ah ain't openin' it," was the rejoinder. "Ah wants th' whole thing, an' Ah don't mean maybe."

Similar scenes were being enacted at the Wheatley Trust Company and at the local Post Office station.

An observer passing up and down the streets would have noted a general exodus from the locality. Moving vans were backed up to apartment houses on nearly every block.

The "For Rent" signs were appearing in larger number in Harlem than at any time in twenty-five years. Landlords looked on helplessly as apartment after apartment emptied and was not filled. Even the refusal to return deposits did not prevent the tenants from moving out. What, indeed, was fifty, sixty or seventy dollars when one was leaving behind insult, ostracism, segregation and discrimination? Moreover, the whitened Negroes were saving a great deal of money by being able to change localities. The mechanics of race prejudice had forced them into the congested Harlem area where, at the mercy of white and black real estate sharks, they had been compelled to pay exorbitant rentals because the demand for housing far exceeded the supply. As a general rule the Negroes were paying one hundred per cent more than white tenants in other parts of the city for a smaller number of rooms and worse service.

The installment furniture and clothing houses in the area were also beginning to feel the results of the activities of Black-No-More, Incorporated. Collectors were reporting their inability to locate certain families or the articles they had purchased on time. Many of the colored folk, it was said, had sold their furniture to second-hand stores and vanished with the proceeds into the great mass of white citizenry.

At the same time there seemed to be more white people on the streets of Harlem than at any time in the past twenty years. Many of them appeared to be on the most intimate terms with the Negroes, laughing, talking, dining and dancing in a most un-Caucasian way. This sort of association had always gone on at night but seldom in the daylight.

Strange Negroes from the West and South who had heard the good news were to be seen on the streets and in public places, patiently awaiting their turn at the Crookman Institute.

Madame Sisseretta Blandish sat disconsolately in an armchair near the front door of her ornate hair-straightening shop, looking blankly at the pedestrians and traffic passing to and fro. These two weeks had been hard ones for her. Everything was going out and nothing coming in. She had been doing very well at her vocation for years and was acclaimed in the

community as one of its business leaders. Because of her prominence as the proprietor of a successful enterprise engaged in
making Negroes appear as much like white folks as possible,
she had recently been elected for the fourth time a Vice-
President of the American Race Pride League. She was also
head of the Woman's Committee of the New York Branch of
the Social Equality League and held an important place in
local Republican politics. But all of these honors brought little or no money with them. They didn't help to pay her rent
or purchase the voluminous dresses she required to drape her
Amazonian form. Only that day her landlord had brought her
the sad news that he either wanted his money or the premises.

Where, she wondered, would she get the money. Like most
New Yorkers she put up a big front with very little cash behind it, always looking hopefully forward to the morrow for
a lucky break. She had two-thirds of the rent money already,
by dint of much borrowing, and if she could "do" a few
nappy heads she would be in the clear; but hardly a customer
had crossed her threshold in a fortnight, except two or three
Jewish girls from downtown who came up regularly to have
their hair straightened because it wouldn't stand inspection
in the Nordic world. The Negro women had seemingly deserted her. Day after day she saw her old customers pass by
hurriedly without even looking in her direction. Verily a
revolution was taking place in Negro society.

"Oh, Miss Simpson!" cried the hair-straightener after a
passing young lady. "Ain't you going to say hello?"

The young woman halted reluctantly and approached the
doorway. Her brown face looked strained. Two weeks before
she would have been a rare sight in the Black Belt because
her kinky hair was not straightened; it was merely combed,
brushed and neatly pinned up. Miss Simpson had vowed that
she wasn't going to spend any dollar a week having her hair
"done" when she only lacked fifteen dollars of having money
enough to quit the Negro race forever.

"Sorry, Mrs. Blandish," she apologized, "but I swear I

didn't see you. I've been just that busy that I haven't had eyes
for anything or anybody except my job and back home again.
You know I'm all alone now. Yes, Charlie went over two
weeks ago and I haven't heard a word from him. Just think
of that! After all I've done for that nigger. Oh well! I'll soon
be over there myself. Another week's work will fix me all
right."

"Humph!" snorted Mme. Blandish. "That's all you niggers are thinking about nowadays. Why don't you come
down here and give me some business? If I don't hurry up
and make some more money I'll have to close up this place
and go to work myself."

"Well, I'm sorry, Mrs. Blandish," the girl mumbled indifferently, moving off toward the corner to catch the approaching street car, "but I guess I can hold out with this here bad
hair until Saturday night. You know I've taken too much
punishment being dark these twenty-two years to miss this
opportunity. . . . Well," she flung over her shoulder, "Good-
bye! See you later."

Madame Blandish settled her 250 pounds back into her
armchair and sighed heavily. Like all American Negroes she
had desired to be white when she was young and before she
entered business for herself and became a person of conse-
quence in the community. Now she had lived long enough
to have no illusions about the magic of a white skin. She liked
her business and she liked her social position in Harlem. As
a white woman she would have to start all over again, and
she wasn't so sure of herself. Here at least she was somebody.
In the great Caucasian world she would be just another white
woman, and they were becoming a drug on the market, what
with the simultaneous decline of chivalry, the marriage rate
and professional prostitution. She had seen too many elderly,
white-haired Caucasian females scrubbing floors and toiling
in sculleries not to know what being just another white
woman meant. Yet she admitted to herself that it would be
nice to get over being the butt for jokes and petty prejudice.

The Madame was in a quandary and so also were hundreds of others in the upper stratum of Harlem life. With the Negro masses moving out from under them, what other alternative did they have except to follow? True, only a few hundred Negroes had so far vanished from their wonted haunts, but it was known that thousands, tens of thousands, yes, millions would follow them.

FOUR

Matthew Fisher, alias Max Disher, joined the Easter Sunday crowds, twirling his malacca stick and ogling the pretty flappers who passed giggling in their spring finery. For nearly three months he had idled around the Georgia capital hoping to catch a glimpse of the beautiful girl who on New Year's Eve had told him "I never dance with niggers." He had searched diligently in almost every stratum of Atlanta society, but he had failed to find her. There were hundreds of tall, beautiful, blonde maidens in the city; to seek a particular one whose name one did not know was somewhat akin to hunting for a Russian Jew in the Bronx or a particular Italian gunman in Chicago.

For three months he had dreamed of this girl, carefully perused the society columns of the local newspapers on the chance that her picture might appear in them. He was like most men who have been repulsed by a pretty girl, his desire for her grew stronger and stronger.

He was not finding life as a white man the rosy existence he had anticipated. He was forced to conclude that it was pretty dull and that he was bored. As a boy he had been taught to look up to white folks as just a little less than gods; now he found them little different from the Negroes, except that they were uniformly less courteous and less interesting.

Often when the desire for the happy-go-lucky, jovial goodfellowship of the Negroes came upon him strongly, he would go down to Auburn Avenue and stroll around the vicinity, looking at the dark folk and listening to their conversation and banter. But no one down there wanted him around. He was a white man and thus suspect. Only the black women who ran the "Call Houses" on the hill wanted his company. There was nothing left for him except the hard, materialistic, grasping, inbred society of the whites. Sometimes a slight feeling of regret that he had left his people forever would cross his mind, but it fled before the painful memories of past experiences in this, his home town.

The unreasoning and illogical color prejudice of most of the people with whom he was forced to associate infuriated him. He often laughed cynically when some coarse, ignorant white man voiced his opinion concerning the inferior mentality and morality of the Negroes. He was moving in white society now and he could compare it with the society he had known as a Negro in Atlanta and Harlem. What a let-down it was from the good breeding, sophistication, refinement and gentle cynicism to which he had become accustomed as a popular young man about town in New York's Black Belt. He was not able to articulate this feeling but he was conscious of the reaction nevertheless.

For a week, now, he had been thinking seriously of going to work. His thousand dollars had dwindled to less than a hundred. He would have to find some source of income and yet the young white men with whom he talked about work all complained that it was very scarce. Being white, he finally concluded, was no Open Sesame to employment for he sought work in banks and insurance offices without success.

During his period of idleness and soft living, he had followed the news and opinion in the local daily press and confessed himself surprised at the antagonistic attitude of the newspapers toward Black-No-More, Incorporated. From the vantage point of having formerly been a Negro, he was able to see how the newspapers were fanning the color prejudice of the white people. Business men, he found were also bitterly opposed to Dr.

Crookman and his efforts to bring about chromatic democracy in the nation.

The attitude of these people puzzled him. Was not Black-No-More getting rid of the Negroes upon whom all of the blame was placed for the backwardness of the South? Then he recalled what a Negro street speaker had said one night on the corner of 138th Street and Seventh Avenue in New York: that unorganized labor meant cheap labor; that the guarantee of cheap labor was an effective means of luring new industries into the South; that so long as the ignorant white masses could be kept thinking of the menace of the Negro to Caucasian race purity and political control, they would give little thought to labor organization. It suddenly dawned upon Matthew Fisher that this Black-No-More treatment was more of a menace to white business than to white labor. And not long afterward he became aware of the money-making possibilities involved in the present situation.

How could he work it? He was not known and he belonged to no organization. Here was a veritable gold mine but how could he reach the ore? He scratched his head over the problem but could think of no solution. Who would be interested in it that he could trust?

He was pondering this question the Monday after Easter while breakfasting in an armchair restaurant when he noticed an advertisement in a newspaper lying in the next chair. He read it and then re-read it.

THE KNIGHTS OF NORDICA
WANT 10,000 ATLANTA WHITE MEN AND WOMEN TO
JOIN IN THE FIGHT FOR WHITE RACE INTEGRITY.

IMPERIAL KLONKLAVE TONIGHT

THE RACIAL INTEGRITY OF THE CAUCASIAN RACE
IS BEING THREATENED BY THE ACTIVITIES OF A
SCIENTIFIC BLACK BEELZEBUB IN NEW YORK

Let us Unite Now Before It Is
too late!

Come to Nordica Hall Tonight Admission Free.
Rev. Henry Givens,
Imperial Grand Wizard

Here, Matthew figured, was just what he had been looking for. Probably he could get in with this fellow Givens. He
finished his cup of coffee, lit a cigar and, paying his check,
strolled out into the sunshine of Peachtree Street.

He took the trolley out to Nordica Hall. It was a big, un-
painted barnlike edifice, with a suite of offices in front and
a huge auditorium in the rear. A new oilcloth sign reading
THE KNIGHTS OF NORDICA was stretched across the front of
the building.

Matthew paused for a moment and sized up the edifice.
Givens must have some money, he thought, to keep up such
a large place. Might not be a bad idea to get a little dope on
him before going inside.

"This fellow Givens is a pretty big guy around here, ain't
he?" he asked the young man at the soda fountain across the
street.

"Yessah, he's one o' th' bigges' men in this heah town.
Used to be a big somethin' or other in th' old Ku Klux Klan
'fore it died. Now he's stahtin' this heah Knights o' Nordica."

"He must have pretty good jack," suggested Matthew.

"He oughtta have," answered the soda jerker. "My paw
tells me he was close to th' money when he was in th' Klan."

Here, thought Matthew, was just the place for him. He
paid for his soda and walked across the street to the door
marked "Office." He felt a slight tremor of uneasiness as he
turned the knob and entered. Despite his white skin he still
possessed the fear of the Klan and kindred organizations
possessed by most Negroes.

A rather pretty young stenographer asked him his business

as he walked into the ante room. Better be bold, he thought. This was probably the best chance he would have to keep from working, and his funds were getting lower and lower.

"Please tell Rev. Givens, the Imperial Grand Wizard, that Mr. Matthew Fisher of the New York Anthropological Society is very anxious to have about a half-hour's conversation with him relative to his new venture." Matthew spoke in an impressive, businesslike manner, rocked back on his heels and looked profound.

"Yassah," almost whispered the awed young lady, "I'll tell him." She withdrew into an inner office and Matthew chuckled softly to himself. He wondered if he could impress this old fakir as easily as he had the girl.

Rev. Henry Givens, Imperial Grand Wizard of the Knights of Nordica, was a short, wizened, almost-bald, bull-voiced, ignorant ex-evangelist, who had come originally from the hilly country north of Atlanta. He had helped in the organization of the Ku Klux Klan following the Great War and had worked with a zeal only equalled by his thankfulness to God for escaping from the precarious existence of an itinerant saver of souls.

Not only had the Rev. Givens toiled diligently to increase the prestige, power and membership of the defunct Ku Klux Klan, but he had also been a very hard worker in withdrawing as much money from its treasury as possible. He convinced himself, as did the other officers, that this stealing was not stealing at all but merely appropriation of rightful reward for his valuable services. When the morons finally tired of supporting the show and the stream of ten-dollar memberships declined to a trickle, Givens had been able to retire gracefully and live on the interest of his money.

Then, when the newspapers began to recount the activities of Black-No-More, Incorporated, he saw a vision of work to be done, and founded the Knights of Nordica. So far there were only a hundred members but he had high hopes for the future. Tonight, he felt would tell the story. The prospect of a full treasury to dip into again made his little gray eyes twinkle and the palms of his skinny hands itch.

The stenographer interrupted him to announce the new-comer.

"Hum-n!" said Givens, half to himself. "New York Anthropological Society, eh? This feller must know somethin'. Might be able to use him in this business. . . . All right, show him in!"

The two men shook hands and swiftly appraised each other. Givens waved Matthew to a chair.

"How can I serve you, Mr. Fisher?" he began in sepulchral tone dripping with unction.

"It is rather," countered Matthew in his best salesman's croon, "how I can serve you and your valuable organization. As an anthropologist, I have, of course, been long interested in the work with which you have been identified. It has always seemed to me that there was no question in American life more important than that of preserving the integrity of the white race. We all know what has been the fate of those nations that have permitted their blood to be polluted with that of inferior breeds." (He had read some argument like that in a Sunday supplement not long before, which was the extent of his knowledge of anthropology.) "This latest menace of Black-No-More is the most formidable the white people of America have had to face since the founding of the Republic. As a resident of New York City, I am aware, of course, of the extent of the activities of this Negro Crookman and his two associates. Already thousands of blacks have passed over into the white race. Not satisfied with operating in New York City, they have opened their sanitariums in twenty other cities from Coast to Coast. They open a new one almost every day. In their literature and advertisements in the darky newspapers they boast that they are now turning four thousand Negroes white every day." He knitted his blond eyebrows. "You see how great the menace is? At this rate there will not be a Negro in the country in ten years, for you must remember that the rate is increasing every day as new sanitariums are opened. Don't you see that something must be done about this immediately? Don't you see that Congress must be aroused; that these places must be closed?" The young man glared with belligerent indignation.

Rev. Givens saw. He nodded his head as Matthew, now glorying in his newly-discovered eloquence, made point after point, and concluded that this pale, dapper young fellow, with his ready tongue, his sincerity, his scientific training and knowledge of the situation, ought to prove a valuable asset to the Knights of Nordica.

"I tried to interest some agencies in New York," Matthew continued, "but they are all blind to this menace and to their duty. Then someone told me of you and your valuable work, and I decided to come down here and have a talk with you. I had intended to suggest the organization of some such militant secret order as you have started, but since you've already seen the necessity for it, I want to hasten to offer my services as a scientific man and one familiar with the facts and able to present them to your members."

"I should be very glad," boomed Givens, "very happy, indeed, Brother Fisher, to have you join us. We need you. I believe you can help us a great deal. Would you, er—ah, be interested in coming out to the mass meeting this evening? It would help us tremendously to get members if you would be willing to get up and tell the audience what you have just related about the progress of this iniquitous nigger corporation in New York."

Matthew pretended to think over the matter for a moment or two and then agreed. If he made a hit at the initial meeting, he would be sure to get on the staff. Once there he could go after the larger game. Unlike Givens, he had no belief in the racial integrity nonsense nor any confidence in the white masses whom he thought were destined to flock to the Knights of Nordica. On the contrary he despised and hated them. He had the average Negro's justifiable fear of the poor

whites and only planned to use them as a stepladder to the
real money.

When Matthew left, Givens congratulated himself upon
the fact that he had been able to attract such talent to the
organization in its very infancy. His ideas must be sound, he
concluded, if scientists from New York were impressed by
them. He reached over, pulled the dictionary stand toward
him and opened the big book at A.

"Lemme see, now," he muttered aloud. "Anthropology.
Better git that word straight 'fore I go talkin' too much about
it. . . . Humn! Humn! . . . That boy must know a hull lot."
He read over the definition of the word twice without understanding it, and then, cutting off a large chew of tobacco
from his plug, he leaned back in his swivel chair to rest after
the unaccustomed mental exertion.

Matthew went gaily back to his hotel. "Man alive!" he
chortled to himself. "What a lucky break! Can't keep old
Max down long. . . . Will I speak to 'em? Well, I won't stay
quiet!" He felt so delighted over the prospect of getting close
to some real money that he treated himself to an expensive
dinner and a twenty-five-cent cigar. Afterward he inquired
further about old man Givens from the house detective, a
native Atlantan.

"Oh, he's well heeled—the old crook!" remarked the detective. "Damnify could ever understand how such ignorant
people get a-hold of th' money; but there y'are. Owns as
pretty a home as you can find around these parts an' damn
'f he ain't stahtin' a new racket."

"Do you think he'll make anything out of it?" inquired
Matthew, innocently.

"Say, Brother, you mus' be a stranger in these parts. These
damn, ignorant crackers will fall fer anything fer a while.
They ain't had no Klan here fer goin' on three years. Least-
wise it ain't been functionin'." The old fellow chuckled and
spat a stream of tobacco juice into a nearby cuspidor. Matthew sauntered away. Yes, the pickings ought to be good.

Equally enthusiastic was the Imperial Grand Wizard when he came home to dinner that night. He entered the house humming one of his favorite hymns and his wife looked up from the evening paper with surprise on her face. The Rev. Givens was usually something of a grouch but tonight he was as happy as a pickpocket at a country fair.

"What's th' mattah with you?" she inquired, sniffing suspiciously.

"Oh, Honey," he gurgled, "I think this here Knights of Nordica is going over big; going over big! My fame is spreading. Only today I had a long talk with a famous anthropologist from New York and he's going to address our mass meeting tonight."

"Whut's an anthropologist?" asked Mrs. Givens, wrinkling her seamy brow.

"Oh-er, well, he's one of these here scientists what knows all about this here business what's going on up there in New York where them niggers is turning each other white," explained Rev. Givens hastily but firmly. "He's a mighty smaht feller and I want you and Helen to come out and hear him."

"B'lieve Ah will," declared Mrs. Givens, "if this heah rheumatism'll le' me foh a while. Doan know 'bout Helen, though. Evah since that gal went away tuh school she ain't bin int'rested in nuthin' upliftin'!"

Mrs. Givens spoke in a grieved tone and heaved her narrow chest in a deep sigh. She didn't like all this newfangled foolishness of these young folks. They were getting away from God, that's what they were, and she didn't like it. Mrs. Givens was a Christian. There was no doubt about it because she freely admitted it to everybody, with or without provocation. Of course she often took the name of the Creator in vain when she got to quarreling with Henry; she had the reputation among her friends of not always stating the exact truth; she hated Negroes; her spouse had made bitter and profane comment concerning her virginity on their wedding night; and as head of the ladies' auxiliary of the defunct Klan she had copied her husband's financial methods; but that she was a devout Christian no one doubted. She believed the Bible from cover to cover, except what it said about people with money, and she read it every evening aloud, greatly to the annoyance of the Imperial Grand Wizard and his modern and comely daughter.

Mrs. Givens had probably once been beautiful but the wear and tear of a long life as the better half of an itinerant evangelist was apparent. Her once flaming red hair was turning gray and roanlike, her hatchet face was a criss-cross of wrinkles and lines, she was round-shouldered, hollow-chested, walked with a stoop and her long, bony, white hands looked like claws. She alternately dipped snuff and smoked an evil-smelling clay pipe, except when there was company at the house. At such times Helen would insist her mother "act like civilized people."

Helen was twenty and quite confident that she herself was civilized. Whether she was or not, she was certainly beautiful. Indeed, she was such a beauty that many of the friends of the family insisted that she must have been adopted. Taller than either of her parents, she was stately, erect, well proportioned, slender, vivid and knew how to wear her clothes. In only one way did she resemble her parents and that was in things intellectual. Any form of mental effort, she complained, made her head ache, and so her parents had always let her have her way about studying.

At the age of eleven she had been taken from the third grade in public school and sent to an exclusive seminary for the double purpose of gaining social prestige and concealing her mental incapacity. At sixteen when her instructors had about despaired of her, they were overjoyed by the decision of her father to send the girl to a "finishing school" in the North. The "finishing school" about finished what intelligence Helen possessed; but she came forth, four years later, more beautiful, with a better knowledge of how to dress and how to act in exclusive society, enough superficialities to enable her to get by in the "best" circles and a great deal of that shallow facetiousness that passes for sophistication in American upper-class life. A winter in Manhattan had rounded out her education. Now she was back home, thoroughly ashamed of her grotesque parents, and, like the other girls of her set, anxious to get a husband who at the same time was handsome, intelligent, educated, refined and rolling in wealth. As she was ignorant of the fact that no such man existed, she looked confidently forward into the future.

"I don't care to go down there among all those gross people," she informed her father at the dinner table when he broached the subject of the meeting. "They're so crude and elemental, don't you know," she explained, arching her narrow eyebrows.

"The common people are the salt of the earth," boomed Rev. Givens. "If it hadn't been for the common people we wouldn't have been able to get this home and send you off to school. You make me sick with all your modern ideas. You'd do a lot better if you'd try to be more like your Ma."

Both Mrs. Givens and Helen looked quickly at him to see if he was smiling. He wasn't.

"Why don'tcha go, Helen?" pleaded Mrs. Givens. "Yo fathah sez this heah man f'm N'Yawk is uh—uh scientist or somethin' an' knows a whole lot about things. Yuh might l'arn somethin'. Ah'd go mys'f if 'twasn't fo mah rheumatism." She sighed in self-pity and finished gnawing a drumstick.

Helen's curiosity was aroused and although she didn't like the idea of sitting among a lot of mill hands, she was anxious to see and hear this reputedly brilliant young man from the great metropolis where not long before she had lost both her provincialism and chastity.

"Oh, all right," she assented with mock reluctance. "I'll go."

The Knights of Nordica's flag-draped auditorium slowly filled. It was a bare, cavernous structure, with sawdust on the floor, a big platform at one end, row after row of folding wooden chairs and illuminated by large, white lights hanging from the rafters. On the platform was a row of five chairs, the center one being high-backed and gilded. On the lectern downstage was a bulky Bible. A huge American flag was stretched across the rear wall.

The audience was composed of the lower stratum of white working people: hard-faced, lantern-jawed, dull-eyed adult children, seeking like all humanity for something permanent in the eternal flux of life. The young girls in their cheap finery with circus makeup on their faces; the young men, aged before their time by child labor and a violent environment; the middle-aged folk with their shiny, shabby garb and beaten countenances; all ready and eager to be organized for any purpose except improvement of their intellects and standard of living.

Rev. Givens opened the meeting with a prayer "for the success, O God, of this thy work, to protect the sisters and wives and daughters of these, thy people, from the filthy pollution of an alien race."

A choir of assorted types of individuals sang "Onward Christian Soldiers" earnestly, vociferously and badly.

They were about to file off the platform when the song leader, a big, beefy, jovial mountain of a man, leaped upon the stage and restrained them.

"Wait a minute, folks, wait a minute," he commanded. Then turning to the assemblage: "Now people let's put some pep into this. We wanna all be happy and get in th' right spirit for this heah meetin'. Ah'm gonna ask the choir to sing th' first and last verses ovah ag'in, and when they come to th' chorus, Ah wantcha to all join in. Doan be 'fraid. Jesus wouldn't be 'fraid to sing 'Onward Christian Soldiers,' now would he? Come on, then. All right, choir, you staht; an' when Ah wave mah han' you'll join in on that theah chorus."

They obediently followed his directions while he marched up and down the platform, red-faced and roaring and waving his arms in time. When the last note had died away, he dismissed the choir and stepping to the edge of the stage he leaned far out over the audience and barked at them again.

"Come on, now, folks! Yuh can't slow up on Jesus now. He won't be satisfied with jus' one ole measly song. Yuh gotta let 'im know that yuh love 'im; that y're happy an' contented; that yuh ain't got no troubles an' ain't gonna have any. Come on, now. Le's sing that ole favorite what yo'all like so well: 'Pack Up Your Troubles in Your Old Kit Bag and Smile, Smile, Smile.'" He bellowed and they followed him. Again the vast hall shook with sound. He made them rise and grasp each other by the hand until the song ended.

Matthew, who sat on the platform alongside old man Givens viewed the spectacle with amusement mingled with amazement. He was amused because of the similarity of this meeting to the religious orgies of the more ignorant Negroes and amazed that earlier in the evening he should have felt any qualms about lecturing to these folks on anthropology, a subject with which neither he nor his hearers were acquainted. He quickly saw that these people would believe anything that was shouted at them loudly and convincingly enough. He knew what would fetch their applause and bring in their memberships and he intended to repeat it over and over.

The Imperial Grand Wizard spent a half-hour introducing the speaker of the evening, dwelt upon his supposed scholastic attainments, but took pains to inform them that, despite Matthew's vast knowledge, he still believed in the Word of God, the sanctity of womanhood and the purity of the white race.

For an hour Matthew told them at the top of his voice what they believed: i.e., that a white skin was a sure indication of the possession of superior intellectual and moral qualities; that all Negroes were inferior to them; that God had intended for the United States to be a white man's country and that with His help they could keep it so; that their sons and brothers might inadvertently marry Negresses or, worse,

their sisters and daughters might marry Negroes, if
Black-No-More, Incorporated, was permitted to continue its
dangerous activities.

For an hour he spoke, interrupted at intervals by enthusiastic gales of applause, and as he spoke his eye wandered
over the females in the audience, noting the comeliest ones.
As he wound up with a spirited appeal for eager soldiers to
join the Knights of Nordica at five dollars per head and the
half-dozen "planted" emissaries led the march of suckers to
the platform, he noted for the first time a girl who sat in the
front row and gazed up at him raptly.

She was a titian blonde, well-dressed, beautiful and
strangely familiar. As he retired amid thunderous applause
to make way for Rev. Givens and the money collectors, he
wondered where he had seen her before. He studied her from
his seat.

Suddenly he knew. It was she! The girl who had spurned
him; the girl he had sought so long; the girl he wanted more
than anything in the world! Strange that she should be here.
He had always thought of her as a refined, educated and
wealthy lady, far above associating with such people as these.
He was in a fever to meet her, some way, before she got out
of his sight again, and yet he felt just a little disappointed to
find her here.

He could hardly wait until Givens seated himself again
before questioning him as to the girl's identity. As the beefy
song leader led the roaring of the popular closing hymn, he
leaned toward the Imperial Grand Wizard and shouted:
"Who is that tall golden-haired girl sitting in the front row?
Do you know her?"

Rev. Givens looked out over the audience, craning his
skinny neck and blinking his eyes. Then he saw the girl, sitting within twenty feet of him.

"You mean that girl sitting right in front, there?" he asked,
pointing.

"Yes, that one," said Matthew, impatiently.

"Heh! Heh! Heh!" chuckled the Wizard, rubbing his stubbly chin. "Why that there's my daughter, Helen. Like to meet her?"

Matthew could hardly believe his ears. Givens's daughter! Incredible! What a coincidence! What luck! Would he like to meet her? He leaned over and shouted "Yes."

FIVE

A huge silver monoplane glided gracefully to the surface of Mines Field in Los Angeles and came to a pretty stop after a short run. A liveried footman stepped out of the forward compartment armed with a stool which he placed under the rear door. Simultaneously a high-powered foreign car swept up close to the airplane and waited. The rear door of the airplane opened, and to the apparent surprise of the nearby mechanics a tall, black, distinguished-looking Negro stepped out and down to the ground, assisted by the hand of the footman. Behind him came a pale young man and woman, evidently secretaries. The three entered the limousine which rapidly drove off.

"Who's that coon?" asked one of the mechanics, round-eyed and respectful, like all Americans, in the presence of great wealth.

"Don't you know who that is?" inquired another, pityingly. "Why that's that Dr. Crookman. You know, the fellow what's turnin' niggers white. See that B N M on the side of his plane? That stands for Black-No-More. Gee, but I wish I had just half the jack he's made in the last six months!"

"Why I thought from readin' th' papers," protested the first speaker, "that th' law had closed up his places and put 'im outta business."

"Oh, that's a lotta hockey," said the other fellow. "Why

just yesterday th' newspapers said that Black-No-More was openin' a place on Central Avenue. They already got one in Oakland, so a coon told me yesterday."

"'Sfunny," ventured a third mechanic, as they wheeled the big plane into a nearby hangar, "how he don't have nuthin' but white folks around him. He must not like nigger help. His chauffeur's white, his footman's white an' that young gal and feller what was with him are white."

"How do you know?" challenged the first speaker. "They may be darkies that he's turned into white folks."

"That's right," the other replied. "It's gittin' so yuh can't tell who's who. I think that there Knights of Nordica ought to do something about it. I joined up with 'em two months ago but they ain't done nuthin' but sell me an ole uniform an' hold a coupla meetin's."

They lapsed into silence. Sandol, the erstwhile Senegalese, stepped from the cockpit grinning. "Ah, zese Americains," he muttered to himself as he went over the engine, examining everything minutely.

"Where'd yuh come from, buddy?" asked one of the mechanics.

"Den-vair," Sandol replied.

"Whatcha doin', makin' a trip around th' country?" queried another.

"Yes, we air, what you callem, on ze tour inspectione," the aviator continued. They could think of no more to say and soon strolled off.

Around the oval table on the seventh floor of a building on Central Avenue sat Dr. Junius Crookman, Hank Johnson, Chuck Foster, Ranford the Doctor's secretary and four other men. At the lower end of the table Miss Bennett, Ranford's stenographer, was taking notes. A soft-treading waiter whose Negro nature was only revealed by his mocking obsequiousness, served each with champagne.

"To our continued success!" cried the physician, lifting his glass high.

"To our continued success!" echoed the others.

They drained their glasses, and returned them to the polished surface of the table.

"Dog bite it, Doc!" blurted Johnson. "Us sho is doin' fine. Ain't had a bad break since we stahted, an' heah 'tis th' fust o' September."

"Don't holler too soon," cautioned Foster. "The opposition is growing keener every day. I had to pay seventy-five thousand dollars more for this building than it's worth."

"Well, yuh got it, didn't yuh?" asked Johnson. "Just like Ah allus say: when yuh got money yuh kin git anything in this man's country. Whenever things look tight jes pull out th' ole check book an' eve'ything's all right."

"Optimist!" grunted Foster.

"I ain't no pess'mist," Johnson accused.

"Now gentlemen," Dr. Crookman interrupted, clearing his throat, "let's get down to business. We have met here, as you know, not only for the purpose of celebrating the opening of this, our fiftieth sanitarium, but also to take stock of our situation. I have before me here a detailed report of our business affairs for the entire period of seven months and a half that we've been in operation.

"During that time we have put into service fifty sanitariums from Coast to Coast, or an average of one every four and one-half days, the average capacity of each sanitarium being one hundred and five patients. Each place has a staff of six physicians and twenty-four nurses, a janitor, four orderlies, two electricians, bookkeeper, cashier, stenographer and record clerk, not counting four guards.

"For the past four months we have had an equipment factory in Pittsburgh in full operation and a chemical plant in Philadelphia. In addition to this we have purchased four airplanes and a radio broadcasting station. Our expenditures for real estate, salaries and chemicals have totaled six million, two hundred and fifty-five thousand, eighty-five dollars and ten cents. . . ."

"He! He!" chuckled Johnson. "Dat ten cents mus' be fo' one o' them bad ceegars that Fostah smokes."

"Our total income," continued Dr. Crookman, frowning slightly at the interruption, "has been eighteen million, five hundred thousand, three hundred dollars, or three hundred and seventy thousand and six patients at fifty dollars apiece. I think that vindicates my contention at the beginning that the fee should be but fifty dollars—within the reach of the rank and file of Negroes." He laid aside his report and added:

"In the next four months we'll double our output and by the end of the year we should cut the fee to twenty-five dollars." He lightly twirled his waxed mustache between his long sensitive fingers and smiled with satisfaction.

"Yes," said Foster, "the sooner we get this business over with the better. We're going to run into a whole lot more opposition from now on than we have so far encountered."

"Why man!" growled Johnson, "we ain't even stahted on dese darkies yet. And when we git thu wi' dese heah, we kin work on them in th' West Indies. Believe me, Ah doan *nevah* want dis graft tuh end."

"Now," continued Dr. Crookman, "I want to say that Mr. Foster deserves great praise for the industry and ingenuity he has shown in purchasing our real estate and Mr. Johnson deserves equally great praise for the efficient manner in which he has kept down the opposition of the various city officials. As you know, he has spent nearly a million dollars in such endeavors and almost as much again in molding legislative sentiment in Washington and the various state capitals. That accounts for the fact that every bill introduced in a legislature or municipal council to put us out of business has died in committee. Moreover, through his corps of secret operatives, who are mostly young women, he has placed numbers of officials and legislators in a position where they cannot openly oppose our efforts."

A smile of appreciation went around the circle.

"We'll have a whole lot to do from now on," commented Foster.

"Yeh, Big Boy," replied the ex-gambler, "an' whut it takes tuh do it Ah ain't got nuthin' else but!"

"Certainly," said the physician, "our friend Hank has not been overburdened with scruples."

"Ah doan know whut dat is, Chief," grinned Johnson, "but Ah knows whut a check book'll do. Even these crackers tone down when Ah talks bucks."

"This afternoon," continued Crookman, "we also have with us our three regional directors, Doctors Henry Dogan, Charles Hinckle and Fred Selden, as well as our chief chemist, Wallace Butts. I thought it would be a good idea to bring you all together for this occasion so we could get better acquainted. We'll just have a word from each of them. They're all good Race men, you know, even if they have, like the rest of our staff, taken the treatment."

For the next three-quarters of an hour the three directors and the chief chemist reported on the progress of their work. At intervals the waiter brought in cold drinks, cigars and cigarettes. Overhead whirred the electric fans. Out of the wide open windows could be seen the panorama of bungalows, pavements, palm trees, trundling street cars and scooting automobiles.

"Lawd! Lawd! Lawd!" Johnson exclaimed at the conclusion of the meeting, going to the window and gazing out over the city. "Jes gimme a coupla yeahs o' dis graft an' Ah'll make Henry Foahd look like a tramp."

Meanwhile, Negro society was in turmoil and chaos. The colored folk, in straining every nerve to get the Black-No-More treatment, had forgotten all loyalties, affiliations and responsibilities. No longer did they flock to the churches on Sundays or pay dues in their numerous fraternal organizations. They had stopped giving anything to the Anti-Lynching campaign.

Santop Licorice, head of the once-flourishing Back-To-Africa Society, was daily raising his stentorian voice in denunciation of the race for deserting his organization.

Negro business was being no less hard hit. Few people were bothering about getting their hair straightened or skin whitened temporarily when for a couple of weeks' pay they could get both jobs done permanently. The immediate result of this change of mind on the part of the Negro public was to almost bankrupt the firms that made the whitening and straightening chemicals. They were largely controlled by canny Hebrews, but at least a half-dozen were owned by Negroes. The rapid decline in this business greatly decreased the revenue of the Negro weekly newspapers who depended upon such advertising for their sustenance. The actual business of hair straightening that had furnished employment to thousands of colored women who would otherwise have had to go back to washing and ironing declined to such an extent that "To Rent" signs hung in front of nine-tenths of the shops.

The Negro politicians in the various Black Belts, grown fat and sleek "protecting" vice with the aid of Negro votes which they were able to control by virtue of housing segregation, lectured in vain about black solidarity, race pride and political emancipation; but nothing stopped the exodus to the white race. Gloomily the politicians sat in their offices, wondering whether to throw up the sponge and hunt the nearest Black-No-More sanitarium or hold on a little longer in the hope that the whites might put a stop to the activities of Dr. Crookman and his associates. The latter, indeed, was their only hope because the bulk of Negroes, saving their dimes and dollars for chromatic emancipation, had stopped gambling, patronizing houses of prostitution or staging Saturday-night brawls. Thus the usual sources of graft vanished. The black politicians appealed to their white masters for succor, of course, but they found to their dismay that most of the latter had been safely bribed by the astute Hank Johnson.

Gone was the almost European atmosphere of every Negro ghetto: the music, laughter, gaiety, jesting and abandon. Instead, one noted the same excited bustle, wild looks and strained faces to be seen in a war time soldier camp, around a new oil district or before a gold rush. The happy-go-lucky Negro of song and story was gone forever and in his stead was a nervous, money-grubbing black, stuffing away coin in socks, impatiently awaiting a sufficient sum to pay Dr. Crookman's fee.

Up from the South they came in increasing droves, besieging the Black-No-More sanitariums for treatment. There were none of these havens in the South because of the hostility of the bulk of white people but there were many all along the border between the two sections, at such places as Washington, D. C., Baltimore, Cincinnati, Louisville, Evansville, Cairo, St. Louis and Denver. The various Southern communities attempted to stem this, the greatest migration of Negroes in the history of the country, but without avail. By train, boat, wagon, bicycle, automobile and foot they trekked to the promised land; a hopeful procession, filtering through the outposts of police and Knights of Nordica volunteer bands. Where there was great opposition to the Negroes' going, there would suddenly appear large quantities of free bootleg liquor and crisp new currency which would make the most vigilant white opponent of Black-No-More turn his head the other way. Hank Johnson seemed to be able to cope with almost every situation.

The national office of the militant Negro organization, the National Social Equality League, was agog. Telephone bells were ringing, mulatto clerks were hustling excitedly back and forth, messenger boys rushed in and out. Located in the Times Square district of Manhattan, it had for forty years carried on the fight for full social equality for the Negro citizens and the immediate abolition of lynching as a national sport. While this organization had to depend to a large extent upon the charity of white folk for its existence, since the blacks had always been more or less skeptical about the program for liberty and freedom, the efforts of the society were not entirely unprofitable. Vistas of immaculate offices spread in every direction from the elevator and footfalls were muffled in thick imitation-Persian rugs. While the large staff of officials was eager to end all oppression and persecution of the Negro, they were never so happy and excited as when a Negro was barred from a theater or fried to a crisp. Then they would leap for telephones, grab telegraph pads and yell for stenographers; smiling through their simulated indignation at the spectacle of another reason for their continued existence and appeals for funds.

Ever since the first sanitarium of Black-No-More, Incorporated, started turning Negroes into Caucasians, the National Social Equality League's income had been decreasing. No dues had been collected in months and subscriptions to the national mouthpiece, *The Dilemma*, had dwindled to almost nothing. Officials, long since ensconced in palatial apartments, began to grow panic-stricken as pay days got farther apart. They began to envision the time when they would no longer be able for the sake of the Negro race to suffer the hardships of lunching on canvasback duck at the Urban Club surrounded by the white dilettante, endure the perils of first-class transatlantic passage to stage Save-Dear-Africa Conferences or undergo the excruciating torture of rolling back and forth across the United States in drawing-rooms to hear each lecture on the Negro problem. On meager salaries of five thousand dollars a year they had fought strenuously and tirelessly to obtain for the Negroes the constitutional rights which only a few thousand rich white folk possessed. And now they saw the work of a lifetime being rapidly destroyed.

Single-handed they felt incapable of organizing an effective opposition to Black-No-More, Incorporated, so they had called a conference of all of the outstanding Negro leaders of the country to assemble at the League's headquarters on December 1, 1933. Getting the Negro leaders together for any purpose except boasting of each other's accomplishments had previously been impossible. As a usual thing they fought each other with a vigor only surpassed by that of their pleas for racial solidarity and unity of action. This situation, however, was unprecedented, so almost all of the representative gentlemen of color to whom invitations had been sent agreed with alacrity to come. To a man they felt that it was time to bury the hatchet before they became too hungry to do any digging.

In a very private inner office of the N. S. E. L. suite, Dr. Shakespeare Agamemnon Beard, founder of the League and a graduate of Harvard, Yale and Copenhagen (whose haughty bearing never failed to impress both Caucasians and Negroes), sat before a glass-topped desk, rubbing now his curly gray head, and now his full spade beard. For a mere six thousand dollars a year, the learned doctor wrote scholarly and biting editorials in *The Dilemma* denouncing the Caucasians whom he secretly admired and lauding the greatness of the Negroes whom he alternately pitied and despised. In limpid prose he told of the sufferings and privations of the downtrodden black workers with whose lives he was totally and thankfully unfamiliar. Like most Negro leaders, he deified the black woman but abstained from employing aught save octoroons. He talked at white banquets about "we of the black race" and admitted in books that he was part-French, part-Russian, part-Indian and part-Negro. He bitterly denounced the Nordics for debauching Negro women while taking care to hire comely yellow stenographers with weak resistance. In a real way, he loved his people. In time of peace he was a Pink Socialist but when the clouds of war gathered he bivouacked at the feet of Mars.

Before the champion of the darker races lay a neatly typed resolution drawn up by him and his staff the day before and addressed to the Attorney General of the United States. The staff had taken this precaution because no member of it believed that the other Negro leaders possessed sufficient education to word the document effectively and grammatically. Dr. Beard re-read the resolution and then, placing it in the drawer of the desk, pressed one of a row of buttons. "Tell them to come in," he directed. The mulattress turned and switched out of the room, followed by the appraising and approving eye of the aged scholar. He heaved a regretful sigh as the door closed and his thoughts dwelt on the vigor of his youth.

In three or four minutes the door opened again and several well-dressed blacks, mulattoes and white men entered the large office and took seats around the wall. They greeted each other and the President of the League with usual cordiality but for the first time in their lives they were sincere about it. If anyone could save the day it was Beard. They all admitted that, as did the Doctor himself. They pulled out fat cigars, long slender cigarettes and London briar pipes, lit them and awaited the opening of the conference.

The venerable lover of his race tapped with his knuckle for order, laid aside his six-inch cigarette and, rising, said:

"It were quite unseemly for me who lives such a cloistered life and am spared the bane or benefit of many intimate contacts with those of our struggling race who by sheer courage, tenacity and merit have lifted their heads above the mired mass, to deign to take from a more capable individual the unpleasant task of reviewing the combination of unfortunate circumstances that has brought us together, man to man, within the four walls of the office." He shot a foxy glance around the assembly and then went on suavely. "And so, my friends, I beg your august permission to confer upon my able and cultured secretary and confidant, Dr. Napoleon Wellington Jackson, the office of chairman of this temporary body. I need not introduce Dr. Jackson to you. You know of his scholarship, his high sense of duty and his deep love of the suffering black race. You have doubtless had the pleasure of singing some of the many sorrow songs he has written and popularized in the past twenty years, and you must know of his fame as a translator of Latin poets and his authoritative work on the Greek language.

"Before I gratefully yield the floor to Dr. Jackson, however, I want to tell you that our destiny lies in the stars. Ethiopia's fate is in the balance. The Goddess of the Nile weeps bitter tears at the feet of the Great Sphinx. The lowering clouds gather over the Congo and the lightning flashes o'er Togoland. To your tents, O Israel! The hour is at hand."

The President of the N. S. E. L. sat down and the erudite Dr. Jackson, his tall, lanky secretary, got up. There was no fear of Dr. Jackson ever winning a beauty contest. He was a sooty black, very broad shouldered, with long, apelike arms, a diminutive egg-shaped head that sat on his collar like a hen's egg on a demitasse cup and eyes that protruded so far from his head that they seemed about to fall out. He wore pince-nez that were continually slipping from his very flat and oily nose. His chief business in the organization was to write long and indignant letters to public officials and legislators whenever a Negro was mistreated, demanding justice, fair play and other legal guarantees vouchsafed no whites except bloated plutocrats fallen miraculously afoul of the law, and to speak to audiences of sex-starved matrons who yearned to help the Negro stand erect. During his leisure time, which was naturally considerable, he wrote long and learned articles, bristling with references, for the more intellectual magazines, in which he sought to prove conclusively that the plantation shouts of Southern Negro peons were superior to any of Beethoven's symphonies and that the city of Benin was the original site of the Garden of Eden.

"Hhmm! Hu-umn! Now er—ah, gentlemen," began Dr. Jackson, rocking back on his heels, taking off his eye glasses and beginning to polish them with a silk kerchief, "as you know, the Negro race is face to face with a grave crisis. I-ah-presume it is er-ah unnecessary for me to go into any details concerning the-ah activities of Black-No-More, Incorporated. Suffice er-ah umph! ummmmh! to say-ah that it has thrown our society into rather a-ah bally turmoil. Our people are forgetting shamelessly their-ah duty to the-ah organizations that have fought valiantly for them these-ah many years and are now busily engaged chasing a bally-ah will-o-the-wisp. Ahem!

"You-ah probably all fully realize that-ah a continuation of the aforementioned activities will prove disastrous to our-ah organizations. You-ah, like us, must feel-uh that something drastic must be done to preserve the integrity of Negro society. Think, gentlemen, what the future will mean to-uh all those who-uh have toiled so hard for Negro society. What-ah, may I ask, will we do when there are no longer any-ah groups to support us? Of course, Dr. Crookman and-ah his associates have a-uh perfect right to-ah engage in any legitimate business, but-ah their present activities cannot-ah be classed under that head, considering the effect on our endeavors. Before we go any further, however, I-ah would like to introduce our research expert Mr. Walter Williams, who will-ah describe the situation in the South."

Mr. Walter Williams, a tall, heavy-set white man with pale blue eyes, wavy auburn hair and a militant, lantern jaw, rose and bowed to the assemblage and proceeded to paint a heart-rending picture of the loss of pride and race solidarity among Negroes North and South. There was, he said, not a single local of the N. S. E. L. functioning, dues had dwindled to nothing, he had not been able to hold a meeting anywhere, while many of the staunchest supporters had gone over into the white race.

"Personally," he concluded, "I am very proud to be a Negro and always have been (his great-grandfather, it seemed, had been a mulatto), and I'm willing to sacrifice for the uplift of my race. I cannot understand what has come over our people that they have so quickly forgotten the ancient glories of Ethiopia, Songhay and Dahomey, and their

marvelous record of achievement since emancipation." Mr.
Williams was known to be a Negro among his friends and
acquaintances, but no one else would have suspected it.

Another white man of remote Negro ancestry, Rev. Herbert Gronne of Dunbar University, followed the research
expert with a long discourse in which he expressed fear for
the future of his institution whose student body had been
reduced to sixty-five persons and deplored the catastrophe
"that has befallen us black people."

They all listened with respect to Dr. Gronne. He had been
in turn a college professor, a social worker and a minister,
had received the approval of the white folks and was thus
doubly acceptable to the Negroes. Much of his popularity
was due to the fact that he very cleverly knew how to make
statements that sounded radical to Negroes but sufficiently
conservative to satisfy the white trustees of his school. In
addition he possessed the asset of looking perpetually ear-
nest and sincere.

Following him came Colonel Mortimer Roberts, principal
of the Dusky River Agricultural Institute, Supreme General
of the Knights and Daughters of Kingdom Come and president of the Uncle Tom Memorial Association. Colonel Roberts was the acknowledged leader of the conservative Negroes
(most of whom had nothing to conserve) who felt at all times
that the white folks were in the lead and that Negroes should
be careful to guide themselves accordingly.

He was a great mountain of blackness with a head shaped
like an upturned bucket, pierced by two piglike eyes and a
cavernous mouth equipped with large tombstone teeth which
he almost continually displayed. His speech was a cross between the woofing of a bloodhound and the explosion of an
inner tube. It conveyed to most white people an impression
of rugged simplicity and sincerity, which was very fortunate
since Colonel Roberts maintained his school through their
contributions. He spoke as usual about the cordial relations
existing between the two races in his native Georgia, the

effrontery of Negroes who dared whiten themselves and thus disturb the minds of white people and insinuated alliance with certain militant organizations in the South to stop this whitening business before it went too far. Having spoken his mind and received scant applause, the Colonel (some white man had once called him Colonel and the title stuck), puffing and blowing, sat down.

Mr. Claude Spelling, a scared-looking little brown man with big ears, who held the exalted office of president of the Society of Negro Merchants, added his volume of blues to the discussion. The refrain was that Negro business—always anemic—was about to pass out entirely through lack of patronage. Mr. Spelling had for many years been the leading advocate of the strange doctrine that an underpaid Negro worker should go out of his way to patronize a little dingy Negro store instead of going to a cheaper and cleaner chain store, all for the dubious satisfaction of helping Negro merchants grow wealthy.

The next speaker, Dr. Joseph Bonds, a little rat-faced Negro with protruding teeth stained by countless plugs of chewing tobacco and wearing horn-rimmed spectacles, who headed the Negro Data League, almost cried (which would have been terrible to observe) when he told of the difficulty his workers had encountered in their efforts to persuade retired white capitalists, whose guilty consciences persuaded them to indulge in philanthropy, to give their customary donations to the work. The philanthropists seemed to think, said Dr. Bonds, that since the Negroes were busily solving their difficulties, there was no need for social work among them or any collection of data. He almost sobbed aloud when he described how his collections had fallen from $50,000 a month to less than $1000.

His feeling in the matter could easily be appreciated. He was engaged in a most vital and necessary work: i.e., collecting bales of data to prove satisfactorily to all that more money was needed to collect more data. Most of the data were highly informative, revealing the amazing fact that poor people went to jail oftener than rich ones; that most of the people were not getting enough money for their work; that strangely enough there was some connection between poverty, disease and crime. By establishing these facts with mathematical certitude and illustrating them with elaborate graphs, Dr. Bonds garnered many fat checks. For his people, he said, he wanted work, not charity; but for himself he was always glad to get the charity with as little work as possible. For many years he had succeeded in doing so without any ascertainable benefit accruing to the Negro group.

Dr. Bonds's show of emotion almost brought the others to tears and many of them muttered "Yes, Brother" while he was talking. The conferees were getting stirred up but it took the next speaker to really get them excited.

When he rose an expectant hush fell over the assemblage. They all knew and respected the Right Reverend Bishop Ezekiel Whooper of the Ethiopian True Faith Wash Foot Methodist Church for three reasons: viz., his church was rich (though the parishioners were poor), he had a very loud voice and the white people praised him. He was sixty, corpulent and an expert at the art of making cuckolds.

"Our loyal and devoted clergy," he boomed, "are being forced into manual labor and the Negro church is rapidly dying" and then he launched into a violent tirade against Black-No-More and favored any means to put the corporation out of business. In his excitement he blew saliva, waved his long arms, stamped his feet, pummeled the desk, rolled his eyes, knocked down his chair, almost sat on the rug and generally reverted to the antics of Negro bush preachers.

This exhibition proved contagious. Rev. Herbert Gronne, face flushed and shouting amens, marched from one end of

the room to the other; Colonel Roberts, looking like an ine-
briated black-faced comedian, rocked back and forth clap-
ping his hands; the others began to groan and moan. Dr.
Napoleon Wellington Jackson, sensing his opportunity,
began to sing a spiritual in his rich soprano voice. The others immediately joined him. The very air seemed charged
with emotion.

Bishop Whooper was about to start up again, when Dr.
Beard, who had sat cold and disdainful through this out-
break of revivalism, toying with his gold-rimmed fountain
pen and gazing at the exhibition through half-closed eyelids,
interrupted in sharp metallic tones.

"Let's get down to earth now," he commanded. "We've
had enough of this nonsense. We have a resolution here addressed to the Attorney General of the United States demanding that Dr. Crookman and his associates be arrested and
their activities stopped at once for the good of both races.
All those in favor of this resolution say aye. Contrary? . . .
Very well, the ayes have it. . . . Miss Hilton please send off
this telegram at once!"

They looked at Dr. Beard and each other in amazement.
Several started to meekly protest.

"You gentlemen are all twenty-one, aren't you?" sneered
Beard. "Well, then be men enough to stand by your decision."

"But Doctor Beard," objected Rev. Gronne, "isn't this a
rather unusual procedure?"

"Rev. Gronne," the great man replied, "it's not near as
unusual as Black-No-More. I have probably ruffled your dig-
nity but that's nothing to what Dr. Crookman will do."

"I guess you're right, Beard," the college president
agreed.

"I know it," snapped the other.

The Honorable Walter Brybe, who had won his exalted
position as Attorney General of the United States because of
his long and faithful service helping large corporations to
circumvent the federal laws, sat at his desk in Washington,

D. C. Before him lay the weird resolution from the conference of Negro leaders. He pursed his lips and reached for his private telephone.

"Gorman?" he inquired softly into the receiver. "Is that you?"

"Nossuh," came the reply, "this heah is Mistah Gay's valet."

"Well, call Mister Gay to the telephone at once."

"Yassuh."

"That you, Gorman," asked the chief legal officer of the nation addressing the National Chairman of his party.

"Yeh, what's up?"

"You heard 'bout this resolution from them niggers in New York, ain't you? It's been in all of the papers."

"Yes I read it."

"Well, whaddya think we oughtta do about it?"

"Take it easy, Walter. Give 'em the old run around. You know. They ain't got a thin dime; it's this other crowd that's holding the heavy jack. And 'course you know we gotta clean up our deficit. Just lemme work with that Black-No-More crowd. I can talk business with that Johnson fellow."

"All right, Gorman, I think you're right, but you don't want to forget that there's a whole lot of white sentiment against them coons."

"Needn't worry 'bout that," scoffed Gorman. "There's no money behind it much and besides it's in states we can't carry anyhow. Go ahead; stall them New York niggers off. You're a lawyer, you can always find a reason."

"Thanks for the compliment, Gorman," said the Attorney General, hanging up the receiver.

He pressed a button on his desk and a young girl, armed with pencil and pad, came in.

"Take this letter," he ordered: "To Doctor Shakespeare Agamemnon Beard (what a hell of a name!), Chairman of the Committee for the Preservation of Negro Racial Integrity, 1400 Broadway, New York City.

"My dear Dr. Beard:

The Attorney General has received the solution signed by yourself and others and given it careful consideration.

   Regardless of personal views in the matter (I don't give a damn whether they turn white or not, myself) it is not possible for the Department of Justice to interfere with a legitimate business enterprise so long as its methods are within the law. The corporation in question has violated no federal statute and hence there is not the slightest ground for interfering with its activities.

Very truly yours,
WALTER BRYBE.

   "Get that off at once. Give out copies to the press. That's all."

Santop Licorice, founder and leader of the Back-to-Africa Society, read the reply of the Attorney General to the Negro leaders with much malicious satisfaction. He laid aside his morning paper, pulled a fat cigar from a box nearby, lit it and blew clouds of smoke above his woolly head. He was always delighted when Dr. Beard met with any sort of rebuff or embarrassment. He was doubly pleased in this instance because he had been overlooked in the sending out of invitations to Negro leaders to join the Committee for the Preservation of Negro Racial Integrity. It was outrageous, after all the talking he had done in favor of Negro racial integrity.

   Mr. Licorice for some fifteen years had been very profitably advocating the emigration of all the American Negroes to Africa. He had not, of course, gone there himself and had not the slightest intention of going so far from the fleshpots, but he told the other Negroes to go. Naturally the first step in their going was to join his society by paying five dollars a year for membership, ten dollars for a gold, green and purple robe and silver-colored helmet that together cost two dollars and a half, contributing five dollars to the Santop Licorice Defense Fund (there was a perpetual defense fund because Licorice was perpetually in the courts for fraud of some kind), and buying shares at five dollars each in the Royal Black Steamship Company, for obviously one could not get to Africa without a ship and Negroes ought to travel on Negro-owned and operated ships. The ships were Santop's especial pride. True, they had never been to Africa, had never had but one cargo and that, being gin, was half consumed by the unpaid and thirsty crew before the vessel was saved by the Coast Guard, but they had cost more than anything else the Back-To-Africa Society had purchased even though they were worthless except as scrap iron. Mr. Licorice, who was known by his followers as Provisional President of Africa, Admiral of the African Navy, Field Marshal of the African Army and Knight Commander of the Nile, had a genius for being stuck with junk by crafty salesmen. White men only needed to tell him that he was shrewder than white men and he would immediately reach for a check book.

But there was little reaching for check books in his office nowadays. He had been as hard hit as the other Negroes. Why should anybody in the Negro race want to go back to Africa at a cost of five hundred dollars for passage when they could stay in America and get white for fifty dollars? Mr. Licorice saw the point but instead of scuttling back to Demerara from whence he had come to save his race from oppression, he had hung on in the hope that the activities of Black-No-More, Incorporated, would be stopped. In the meantime, he had continued to attempt to save the Negroes by vigorously attacking all of the other Negro organizations and at the same time preaching racial solidarity and coöperation in his weekly newspaper, "*The African Abroad*," which was printed by white folks and had until a year ago been full of skin-whitening and hair-straightening advertisements.

"How is our treasury?" he yelled back through the dingy suite of offices to his bookkeeper, a pretty mulatto.

"What treasury?" she asked in mock surprise.

"Why, I thought we had seventy-five dollars," he blurted.

"We did, but the Sheriff got most of it yesterday or we wouldn't be in here today."

"Huumn! Well, that's bad. And tomorrow's pay day, isn't it?"

"Why bring that up?" she sneered. "I'd forgotten all about it."

"Haven't we got enough for me to get to Atlanta?" Licorice inquired, anxiously.

"There is if you're gonna hitch-hike."

"Well, of course, I couldn't do that," he smiled deprecatingly.

"I should say not," she retorted, surveying his 250-pound, five-feet-six-inches of black blubber.

"Call Western Union," he commanded.

"What with?"

"Over the telephone, of course, Miss Hall," he explained.

"If you can get anything over that telephone you're a better man than I am, Gunga Din."

"Has the service been discontinued, young lady?"

"Try and get a number," she chirped. He gazed ruefully at the telephone.

"Is there anything we can sell?" asked the bewildered Licorice.

"Yeah, if you can get the Sheriff to take off his attachments."

"That's right, I had forgotten."

"You would."

"Please be more respectful, Miss Hall," he snapped. "Somebody might overhear you and tell my wife."

"Which one?" she mocked.

"Shut up," he blurted, touched in a tender spot, "and try to figure out some way for us to get hold of some money."

"You must think I'm Einstein," she said, coming up and perching herself on the edge of his desk.

"Well, if we don't get some operating expenses I won't be able to obtain money to pay your salary," he warned.

"The old songs are the best songs," she wisecracked.

"Oh, come now, Violet," he remonstrated, pawing her buttock, "let's be serious."

"After all these years!" she declared, switching away.

In desperation, he eased his bulk out of the creaking swivel chair, reached for his hat and overcoat and shuffled out of the office. He walked to the curb to hail a taxicab but reconsidered when he recalled that a worn half-dollar was the extent of his funds. Sighing heavily, he trudged the two blocks to the telegraph office and sent a long day letter to Henry Givens, Imperial Grand Wizard of the Knights of Nordica—collect.

"Well, have you figured it out?" asked Violet when he barged into his office again.

"Yes, I just sent a wire to Givens," he replied.

"But he's a nigger-hater, isn't he?" was her surprised comment.

"You want your salary, don't you?" he inquired archly.

"I have for the past month."

"Well, then, don't ask foolish questions," he snapped.

SIX

Two important events took place on Easter Sunday, 1934. The first was a huge mass meeting in the brand-new reinforced concrete auditorium of the Knights of Nordica for the double purpose of celebrating the first anniversary of the militant secret society and the winning of the millionth member. The second event was the wedding of Helen Givens and Matthew Fisher, Grand Exalted Giraw of the Knights of Nordica.

Rev. Givens, the Imperial Grand Wizard of the order, had never regretted that he had taken Fisher into the order and made him his right-hand man. The membership had grown by leaps and bounds, the treasury was bursting with money in spite of the Wizard's constant misappropriation of funds, the regalia factory was running night and day and the influence of the order was becoming so great that Rev. Givens was beginning to dream of a berth in the White House or nearby.

For over six months the order had been publishing *The Warning*, an eight-page newspaper carrying lurid red headlines and poorly-drawn quarterpage cartoons, and edited by Matthew. The noble Southern working people purchased it eagerly, devouring and believing every word in it. Matthew, in 14-point, one-syllable word editorials, painted terrifying pictures of the menace confronting white supremacy and the utter necessity of crushing it. Very cleverly he linked up the Pope, the Yellow Peril, the Alien Invasion and Foreign

Entanglements with Black-No-More as devices of the Devil. He wrote with such blunt sincerity that sometimes he almost persuaded himself that it was all true.

As the money flowed in, Matthew's fame as a great organizer spread throughout the Southland, and he suddenly became the most desirable catch in the section. Beautiful women literally threw themselves at his feet, and, as a former Negro and thus well versed in the technique of amour, he availed himself of all offerings that caught his fancy.

At the same time he was a frequent visitor to the Givens home, especially when Mrs. Givens, whom he heartily detested, was away. From the very first Helen had been impressed by Matthew. She had always longed for the companionship of an educated man, a scientist, a man of literary ability. Matthew to her mind embodied all of these. She only hesitated to accept his first offer of marriage two days after they met because she saw no indication that he had much, if any, money. She softened toward him as the Knights of Nordica treasury grew; and when he was able to boast of a million-dollar bank account, she agreed to marriage and accepted his ardent embraces in the meantime.

And so, before the yelling multitude of night-gowned Knights, they were united in holy wedlock on the stage of the new auditorium. Both, being newlyweds, were happy. Helen had secured the kind of husband she wanted, except that she regretted his association with what she called low-brows; while Matthew had won the girl of his dreams and was thoroughly satisfied, except for a slight regret that her grotesque mother wasn't dead and some disappointment that his spouse was so much more ignorant than she was beautiful.

As soon as Matthew had helped to get the Knights of Nordica well under way with enough money flowing in to satisfy the avaricious Rev. Givens, he had begun to study ways and means of making some money on the side. He had power, influence and prestige and he intended to make good use of them. So he had obtained audiences individually with several of the leading business men of the Georgia capital.

He always prefaced his proposition by pointing out that the working people were never so contented, profits never so high and the erection of new factories in the city never so intensive; that the continued prosperity of Atlanta and of the entire South depended upon keeping labor free from Bolshevism, Socialism, Communism, Anarchism, trade unionism and other subversive movements. Such un-American philosophies, he insisted, had ruined European countries and from their outposts in New York and other Northern cities were sending emissaries to seek a foothold in the South and plant the germ of discontent. When this happened, he warned gloomily, then farewell to high profits and contented labor. He showed copies of books and pamphlets which he had ordered from radical book stores in New York but which he asserted were being distributed to the prospect's employees.

He then explained the difference between the defunct Ku Klux Klan and the Knights of Nordica. While both were interested in public morals, racial integrity and the threatened invasion of America by the Pope, his organization glimpsed its larger duty, the perpetuation of Southern prosperity by the stabilization of industrial relations. The Knights of Nordica, favored by increasing membership, was in a position to keep down all radicalism, he said, and then boldly asserted that Black-No-More was subsidized by the Russian Bolsheviks. Would the gentlemen help the work of the Nordicists along with a small contribution? They would and did. Whenever there was a slump in the flow of cash from this source, Matthew merely had his print shop run off a bale of Communistic tracts which his secret operatives distributed around in the mills and factories. Contributions would immediately increase.

Matthew had started this lucrative side enterprise none too soon. There was much unemployment in the city, wages were being cut and work speeded up. There was dissatisfaction and grumbling among the workers and a small percentage of them was in a mood to give ear to the half-dozen timid organizers of the conservative unions who were being paid to unionize the city but had as yet made no headway. A union might not be so bad after all.

The great mass of white workers, however, was afraid to organize and fight for more pay because of a deepset fear that the Negroes would take their jobs. They had heard of black labor taking the work of white labor under the guns of white militia, and they were afraid to risk it. They had first read of the activities of Black-No-More, Incorporated, with a secret feeling akin to relief but after the orators of the Knights of Nordica and the editorials of *The Warning* began to portray the menace confronting them, they forgot about their economic ills and began to yell for the blood of Dr. Crookman and his associates. Why, they began to argue, one couldn't tell who was who! Herein lay the fundamental cause of all their ills. Times were hard, they reasoned, because there were so many white Negroes in their midst taking their jobs and undermining their American standard of living. None of them had ever attained an American standard of living to be sure, but that fact never occurred to any of them. So they flocked to the meetings of the Knights of Nordica and night after night sat spellbound while Rev. Givens, who had finished the eighth grade in a one-room country school, explained the laws of heredity and spoke eloquently of the growing danger of black babies.

Despite his increasing wealth (the money came in so fast he could scarcely keep track of it), Matthew maintained close contacts with the merchants and manufacturers. He sent out private letters periodically to prominent men in the Southern business world in which he told of the marked psychological change that had come over the working classes of the South since the birth of the K. of N. He told how they had been discontented and on the brink of revolution when his organization rushed in and saved the South. Unionism and such destructive nostrums had been forgotten, he averred, when *The Warning* had revealed the latest danger to the white race. Of course, he always added, such work required large sums of money and contributions from conservative, substantial and public-spirited citizens were ever acceptable. At the end of each letter there appeared a suggestive paragraph pointing out the extent to which the prosperity of the New South was due to its "peculiar institutions" that made the worker race conscious instead of class conscious, and that with the passing of these "peculiar institutions" would also pass prosperity. This reasoning proved very effective, financially speaking.

Matthew's great success as an organizer and his increasing popularity was not viewed by Rev. Givens with equanimity. The former evangelist knew that everybody of intelligence in the upper circles of the order realized that the growth and prosperity of the Knights of Nordica was largely due to the industry, efficiency and intelligence of Matthew. He had been told that many people were saying that Fisher ought to be Imperial Grand Wizard instead of Grand Exalted Giraw.

Givens had the ignorant man's fear and suspicion of anybody who was supposedly more learned than he. His position, he felt, was threatened, and he was decidedly uneasy. He neither said nor did anything about it, but he fretted a great deal to his wife, much to her annoyance. He was consequently overjoyed when Matthew asked him for Helen's hand, and gave his consent with alacrity. When the marriage was consummated, he saw his cup filled to overflowing and no clouds on the horizon. The Knights of Nordica was safe in the family.

One morning a week or two after his wedding, Matthew was sitting in his private office when his secretary announced a caller, one B. Brown. After the usual delay staged for the purpose of impressing all visitors, Matthew ordered him in. A short, plump, well-dressed, soft-spoken man entered and greeted him respectfully. The Grand Exalted Giraw waved to a chair and the stranger sat down. Suddenly, leaning over close to Matthew, he whispered, "Don't recognize me, do you Max?"

The Grand Giraw paled and started. "Who are you?" he whispered hoarsely. How in the devil did this man know him? He peered at him sharply.

The newcomer grinned. "Why it's me, Bunny Brown, you big sap!"

"Well, cut my throat!" Matthew exclaimed in amazement. "Boy, is it really you?" Bunny's black face had miraculously bleached. He seemed now more chubby and cherubic than ever.

"It ain't my brother," said Bunny with his familiar beam.

"Bunny, where've you been all this time? Why didn't you come on down here when I wrote you? You must've been in jail."

"Mind reader! That's just where I've been," declared the former bank clerk.

"What for? Gambling?"

"No: Rambling."

"What do you mean: Rambling?" asked the puzzled Matthew.

"Just what I said, Big Boy. Got to rambling around with a married woman. Old story: husband came in unexpectedly and I had to crown him. The fire escape was slippery and I slipped. Couldn't run after I hit the ground and the flatfoot nabbed me. Got a lucky break in court or I wouldn't be here."

"Was it a white woman?" asked the Grand Exalted Giraw.

"She wasn't black," said Bunny.

"It's a good thing you weren't black, too!"

"Our minds always ran in the same channels," Bunny commented.

"Got any jack?" asked Matthew.

"Is it likely?"

"Do you want a job?"

"No, I prefer a position."

"Well, I think I can fix you up here for about five grand to begin with," said Matthew.

"Santa Claus! What do I have to do: assassinate the President?"

"No, kidder; just be my right-hand man. You know, follow me through thick and thin."

"All right, Max; but when things get too thick, I'm gonna thin out."

"For Christ's sake don't call me Max," cautioned Matthew.

"That's your name ain't it?"

"No, simp. Them days has gone forever. It's Matthew Fisher now. You go pulling that Max stuff and I'll have to answer more questions than a traffic officer."

"Just think," mused Bunny. "I been reading about you right along in the papers but until I recognized your picture in last Sunday's paper I didn't know who you were. Just how long have you been in on this graft?"

"Ever since it started."

"Say not so! You must have a wad of cash salted away by this time."

"Well, I'm not appealing for charity," Matthew smiled sardonically.

"How many squaws you got now?"

"Only one, Bunny—regular."

"What's matter, did you get too old?" chided his friend.

"No, I got married."

"Well, that's the same thing. Who's the unfortunate woman?"

"Old man Givens's girl."

"Judas Priest! You got in on the ground floor, didn't you?"

"I didn't miss. Bunny, old scout, she's the same girl that turned me down that night in the Honky Tonk," Matthew told him with satisfaction.

"Well, hush my mouth! This sounds like a novel," Bunny chuckled.

"Believe it or not, papa, it's what God loves," Matthew grinned.

"Well, you lucky hound! Getting white didn't hurt you none."

"Now listen, Bunny," said Matthew, dropping to a more serious tone, "from now on you're private secretary to the Grand Exalted Giraw; that's me."

"What's a Giraw?"

"I can't tell you; I don't know myself. Ask Givens sometime. He invented it but if he can explain it I'll give you a grand."

"When do I start to work? Or rather, when do I start drawing money?"

"Right now, Old Timer. Here's a century to get you fixed up. You eat dinner with me tonight and report to me in the morning."

"Fathers above!" said Bunny. "Dixie must be heaven."

"It'll be hell for you if these babies find you out; so keep your nose clean."

"Watch me, Mr. Giraw."

"Now listen, Bunny. You know Santop Licorice, don't you?"

"Who doesn't know that hippo?"

"Well, we've had him on our payroll since December. He's fighting Beard, Whooper, Spelling and that crowd. He was on the bricks and we helped him out. Got his paper to appearing regularly, and all that sort of thing."

"So the old crook sold out the race, did he?" cried the amazed Bunny.

"Hold that race stuff, you're not a shine anymore. Are you surprised that he sold out? You're actually becoming innocent," said Matthew.

"Well, what about the African admiral?" Bunny asked.

"This: In a couple of days I want you to run up to New York and look around and see if his retention on the payroll is justified. I got a hunch that nobody is bothering about his paper or what he says, and if that's true we might as well can him; I can use the jack to better advantage."

"Listen here, Boy, this thing is running me nuts. Here you are fighting this Black-No-More, and so is Beard, Whooper, Gronne, Spelling and the rest of the Negro leaders, yet you have Licorice on the payroll to fight the same people that are fighting your enemy. This thing is more complicated than a flapper's past."

"Simple, Bunny, simple. Reason why you can't understand it is because you don't know anything about high strategy."

"High what?" asked Bunny.

"Never mind, look it up at your leisure. Now you can savvy the fact that the sooner these spades are whitened the sooner this graft will fall through, can't you?"

"Righto," said his friend.

"Well, the longer we can make the process, the longer we continue to drag down the jack. Is that clear?"

"As a spring day."

"You're getting brighter by the minute, old man," jeered Matthew.

"Coming from you, that's no compliment."

"As I was saying, the longer it takes, the longer we last. It's my business to see that it lasts a long time but neither do I want it to stop because that also would be disastrous."

Bunny nodded: "You're a wise egg!"

"Thanks, that makes it unanimous. Well, I don't want my side to get such an upper hand that it will put the other side out of business, or vice versa. What we want is a status quo."

"Gee, you've got educated since you've been down here with these crackers."

"You flatter them, Bunny; run along now. I'll have my car come by your hotel to bring you to dinner."

"Thanks for the compliment, old man, but I'm staying at the Y. M. C. A. It's cheaper," laughed Bunny.

"But is it safer?" kidded Matthew, as his friend withdrew.

Two days later Bunny Brown left for New York on a secret

mission. Not only was he to spy on Santop Licorice and see how effective his work was, but he was also to approach Dr. Shakespeare Agamemnon Beard, Dr. Napoleon Wellington Jackson, Rev. Herbert Gronne, Col. Mortimer Roberts, Prof. Charles Spelling, and the other Negro leaders with a view to getting them to speak to white audiences for the benefit of the Knights of Nordica. Matthew already knew that they were in a precarious economic situation since they now had no means of income, both the black masses and the philanthropic whites having deserted them. Their white friends, mostly Northern plutocrats, felt that the race problem was being satisfactorily solved by Black-No-More, Incorporated, and so did the Negroes. Bunny's job was to convince them that it was better to lecture for the K. of N. and grow fat than to fail to get chances to lecture to Negroes who weren't interested in what they said anyhow. The Grand Exalted Giraw had a personal interest in these Negro leaders. He realized that they were too old or too incompetent to make a living except by preaching and writing about the race problem, and since they had lost their influence with the black masses, they might be a novelty to introduce to the K. of N. audiences. He felt that their racial integrity talks would click with the crackers. They knew more about it too than any of his regular speakers, he realized.

As the train bearing Bunny pulled into the station in Charlotte, he bought an evening paper. The headline almost knocked him down:

WEALTHY WHITE GIRL HAS NEGRO BABY

He whistled softly and muttered to himself, "Business picks up from now on." He thought of Matthew's marriage and whistled again.

From that time on there were frequent reports in the daily press of white women giving birth to black babies. In some cases, of course, the white women had recently become white but the blame for the tar-brushed offspring in the public mind always rested on the shoulders of the father, or rather, of the husband. The number of cases continued to increase. All walks of life were represented. For the first time the prevalence of sexual promiscuity was brought home to the thinking people of America. Hospital authorities and physicians had known about it in a general way but it had been unknown to the public.

The entire nation became alarmed. Hundreds of thousands of people, North and South, flocked into the Knights of Nordica. The real white people were panic-stricken, especially in Dixie. There was no way, apparently, of telling a real Caucasian from an imitation one. Every stranger was viewed with suspicion, which had a very salutary effect on the standard of sex morality in the United States. For the first time since 1905, chastity became a virtue. The number of petting parties, greatly augmented by the development of aviation, fell off amazingly. One must play safe, the girls argued.

The holidays of traveling salesmen, business men and fraternal delegates were made less pleasant than of yore. The old orgiastic days in the big cities seemed past for all time. It also suddenly began to dawn upon some men that the pretty young thing they had met at the seashore and wanted to rush to the altar might possibly be a whitened Negress; and young women were almost as suspicious. Rapid-fire courtships and gin marriages declined. Matrimony at last began to be approached with caution. Nothing like this situation had been known since the administration of Grover Cleveland.

Black-No-More, Incorporated, was not slow to seize upon this opportunity to drum up more business. With 100 sanitariums going full blast from Coast to Coast, it now announced in full page advertisements in the daily press that it was establishing lying-in hospitals in the principal cities where all prospective mothers could come to have their babies, and that whenever a baby was born black or mulatto, it would immediately be given the 24-hour treatment that permanently turned black infants white. The country breathed easier, particularly the four million Negroes who had become free because white.

In a fortnight Bunny Brown returned. Over a quart of passable rye, the two friends discussed his mission.

"What about Licorice?" asked Matthew.

"Useless. You ought to give him the gate. He's taking your jack but he isn't doing a thing but getting your checks and eating regularly. His followers are scarcer than Jews in the Vatican."

"Well, were you able to talk business with any of the Negro leaders?"

"Couldn't find any of them. Their offices are all closed and they've moved away from the places where they used to live. Broke, I suppose."

"Did you inquire for them around Harlem?"

"What was the use? All of the Negroes around Harlem nowadays are folks that have just come there to get white; the rest of them left the race a long time ago. Why, Boy, darkies are as hard to find on Lenox Avenue now as they used to be in Tudor City."

"What about the Negro newspapers? Are any of them running still?"

"Nope, they're a thing of the past. Shines are too busy getting white to bother reading about lynching, crime and peonage," said Bunny.

"Well," said Matthew, "it looks as if old Santop Licorice is the only one of the old gang left."

"Yeah, and he won't be black long, now that you're cutting him off the payroll."

"I think he could make more money staying black."

"How do you figure that out?" asked Bunny.

"Well, the dime museums haven't closed down, you know," said Matthew.

SEVEN

One June morning in 1934, Grand Exalted Giraw Fisher received a report from one of his secret operatives in the town of Paradise, South Carolina, saying:

> The working people here are talking about going on strike next week unless Blickdoff and Hortzenboff, the owners of the Paradise Mill, increase pay and shorten hours. The average wage is around fifteen dollars a week, the work day eleven hours. In the past week the company has speeded up the work so much that the help say they cannot stand the pace.
>
> The owners are two Germans who came to this country after the war. They employ 1000 hands, own all of the houses in Paradise and operate all of the stores. Most of the hands belong to the Knights of Nordica and they want the organization to help them unionize. Am awaiting instructions.

Matthew turned to Bunny and grinned. "Here's more money," he boasted, shaking the letter in his assistant's face.

"What can you do about it?" that worthy inquired.

"What can I do? Well, Brother, you just watch my smoke. Tell Ruggles to get the plane ready," he ordered. "We'll fly over there at once."

Two hours later Matthew's plane sat down on the broad, close-clipped lawn in front of the Blickdoff-Hortzenboff cotton mill. Bunny and the Grand Giraw entered the building and walked to the office.

"Whom do you wish to see?" asked a clerk.

"Mr. Blickdoff, Mr. Hortzenboff or both; preferably both," Matthew replied.

"And who's calling?"

"The Grand Exalted Giraw of the Ancient and Honorable Order of the Knights of Nordica and his secretary," boomed that gentleman. The awed young lady retired into an inner sanctum.

"That sure is some title," commented Bunny in an undertone.

"Yes, Givens knows his stuff when it comes to that. The longer and sillier a title, the better the yaps like it."

The young lady returned and announced that the two owners would be glad to receive the eminent Atlantan. Bunny and Matthew entered the office marked "Private."

Hands were shaken, greetings exchanged and then Matthew got right down to business. He had received contributions from these two mill owners so to a certain extent they understood one another.

"Gentlemen," he queried, "is it true that your employees are planning to strike next week?"

"So ve haff heardt," puffed the corpulent, undersized Blickdoff.

"Well, what are you going to do about it?"

"De uszual t'ing, uff coarse," replied Hortzenboff, who resembled a beer barrel on stilts.

"You can't do the usual thing," warned Matthew. "Most of these people are members of the Knights of Nordica. They are looking to us for protection and we mean to give it to them."

"Vy ve t'ought you vas favorable," exclaimed Blickdoff.

"Und villing to be reasonable," added Hortzenboff.

"That's true," Matthew agreed, "but you're squeezing these people too hard."

"But ve can't pay dem any more," protested the squat partner. "Vot ve gonna do?"

"Oh, you fellows can't kid me, I know you're coining the jack; but if you think it's worth ten grand to you, I think I can adjust matters," the Grand Giraw stated.

"Ten t'ousand dollars?" the two mill men gasped.

"You've got good ears," Matthew assured them. "And if you don't come across I'll put the whole power of my organization behind your hands. Then it'll cost you a hundred grand to get back to normal."

The Germans looked at each other incredulously.

"Are you t'reatening us, Meester Fisher?" whined Blickdoff.

"You've got a good head at figuring out things, Blickdoff," Matthew retorted, sarcastically.

"Suppose ve refuse?" queried the heavier Teuton.

"Yeah, suppose you do. Can't you imagine what'll happen when I pull these people off the job?"

"Ve'll call out de militia," warned Blickdoff.

"Don't make me laugh," Matthew commented. "Half the militiamen are members of my outfit."

The Germans shrugged their shoulders hopelessly while Matthew and Bunny enjoyed their confusion.

"How mutch you say you wandt?" asked Hortzenboff.

"Fifteen grand," replied the Grand Giraw, winking at Bunny.

"Budt you joost said ten t'ousand a minute ago," screamed Blickdoff, gesticulating.

"Well, it's fifteen now," said Matthew, "and it'll be twenty grand if you babies don't hurry up and make up your mind."

Hortzenboff reached hastily for the big check book and commenced writing. In a moment he handed Matthew the check.

"Take this back to Atlanta in the plane," ordered Matthew, handing the check to Bunny, "and deposit it. Safety first." Bunny went out.

"You don't act like you trust us," Blickdoff accused.

"Why should I?" the ex-Negro retorted. "I'll just stick

around for a while and keep you two company. You fellows might change your mind and stop payment on that check."

"Ve are honest men, Meester Fisher," cried Hortzenboff.

"Now I'll tell one," sneered the Grand Giraw, seating himself and taking a handful of cigars out of a box on the desk.

The following evening the drab, skinny, hollow-eyed mill folk trudged to the mass meeting called by Matthew in the only building in Paradise not owned by the company—the Knights of Nordica Hall. They poured into the ramshackle building, seated themselves on the wooden benches and waited for the speaking to begin.

They were a sorry lot, under-nourished, bony, vacant-looking, and yet they had seen a dim light. Without suggestion or agitation from the outside world, from which they were almost as completely cut off as if they had been in Siberia, they had talked among themselves and concluded that there was no hope for them except in organization. What they all felt they needed was wise leadership, and they looked to the Knights of Nordica for it, since they were all members of it and there was no other agency at hand. They waited now expectantly for the words of wisdom and encouragement which they expected to hear fall from the lips of their beloved Matthew Fisher, who now looked down upon them from the platform with cynical humor mingled with disgust.

They had not long to wait. A tall, gaunt mountaineer, who acted as chairman, after beseeching the mill hands to stand together like men and women, introduced the Grand Exalted Giraw.

Matthew spoke forcefully and to the point. He reminded them that they were men and women; that they were free, white and twenty-one; that they were citizens of the United States; that America was their country as well as Rockefeller's; that they must stand firm in the defense of their rights as working people; that the worker was worthy of his hire; that nothing should be dearer to them than the maintenance of white supremacy. He insinuated that even in their midst there probably were some Negroes who had been turned white by Black-No-More. Such individuals, he insisted, made poor union material because they always showed their Negro characteristics and ran away in a crisis. Ending with a fervent plea for liberty, justice and a square deal, he sat down amid tumultuous applause. Eager to take advantage of their enthusiasm, the chairman began to call for members. Happily the people crowded around the little table in front of the platform to give their names and pay dues.

Swanson, the chairman and acknowledged leader of the militant element, was tickled with the results of the meeting. He slapped his thighs mountaineer fashion, shifted his chew of tobacco from the right cheek to the left, his pale blue eyes twinkling, and "allowed" to Matthew that the union would soon bring the Paradise Mill owners to terms. The Grand Exalted Giraw agreed.

Two days later, back in Atlanta, Matthew held a conference with a half-dozen of his secret operatives in his office. "Go to Paradise and do your stuff," he commanded, "and do it right."

The next day the six men stepped from the train in the little South Carolina town, engaged rooms at the local hotel and got busy. They let it be known that they were officials of the Knights of Nordica sent from Atlanta by the Grand Exalted Giraw to see that the mill workers got a square deal. They busied themselves visiting the three-room cottages of the workers, all of which looked alike, and talking very confidentially.

In a day or so it began to be noised about that Swanson, leader of the radical element, was really a former Negro from Columbia. It happened that a couple of years previously he had lived in that city. Consequently he readily admitted that he had lived there when asked innocently by one of the strangers in the presence of a group of workers. When Swanson wasn't looking, the questioner glanced significantly at those in the group.

That was enough. To the simple-minded workers Swanson's admission was conclusive evidence that the charge of being a Negro was true. When he called another strike meeting, no one came except a few of Fisher's men. The big fellow was almost ready to cry because of the unexplained falling away of his followers. When one of the secret operatives told him the trouble he was furious.

"Ah haint no damn nigger a-tall," he shouted. "Ah'm a white man an' kin prove hit!"

Unfortunately he could not prove to the satisfaction of his fellow workers that he was not a Negro. They were adamant. On the streets they passed him without speaking and they complained to the foremen at the mill that they didn't want to work with a nigger. Broken and disheartened after a week of vain effort, Swanson was glad to accept carfare out of the vicinity from one of Matthew's men who pretended to be sympathetic.

With the departure of Swanson, the cause of the mill workers was dealt a heavy blow, but the three remaining ringleaders sought to carry on. The secret operatives of the Grand Exalted Giraw got busy again. One of the agitators was asked if it was true that his grandfather was a nigger. He strenuously denied the charge but being ignorant of the identity of his father he could not very well be certain about his grandfather. He was doomed. Within a week the other two were similarly discredited. Rumor was wafted abroad that the whole idea of a strike was a trick of smart niggers in the North who were in the pay of the Pope.

The erstwhile class conscious workers became terror-stricken by the specter of black blood. You couldn't, they said, be sure of anybody any more, and it was better to leave things as they were than to take a chance of being led by some nigger. If the colored gentry couldn't sit in the movies and ride in the trains with white folks, it wasn't right for them to be organizing and leading white folks.

The radicals and laborites in New York City had been

closely watching developments in Paradise ever since the news of the big mass meeting addressed by Matthew was broadcast by the Knights of Nordica news service. When it seemed that the mill workers were, for some mysterious reason, going to abandon the idea of striking, liberal and radical labor organizers were sent down to the town to see what could be done toward whipping up the spirit of revolt.

The representative of the liberal labor organization arrived first and immediately announced a meeting in the Knights of Nordica Hall, the only obtainable place. Nobody came. The man couldn't understand it. He walked out into the town square, approached a little knot of men and asked what was the trouble.

"Y're from that there Harlem in N'Yawk, haint ye?" asked one of the villagers.

"Why yes, I live in Harlem. What about it?"

"Well, we haint a gonna have no damn nigger leadin' us, an' if ye know what's healthy fer yuh yo'll git on away f'um here," stated the speaker.

"Where do you get that nigger stuff?" inquired the amazed and insulted organizer. "I'm a white man."

"Yo ain't th' first white nigger whut's bin aroun' these parts," was the reply.

The organizer, puzzled but helpless, stayed around town for a week and then departed. Somebody had told the simple folk that Harlem was the Negro district in New York, after ascertaining that the organizer lived in that district. To them Harlem and Negro became synonymous and the laborite was doomed.

The radical labor organizer, refused permission to use the Knights of Nordica Hall because he was a Jew, was prevented from holding a street meeting when someone started a rumor that he believed in dividing up property, nationalizing women, and was in addition an atheist. He freely admitted the first, laughed at the second and proudly proclaimed the third. That was sufficient to inflame the mill hands, although

God had been strangely deaf to their prayers, they owned no property to divide and most of their women were so ugly that they need have had no fears that any outsiders would want to nationalize them. The disciple of Lenin and Trotsky vanished down the road with a crowd of emaciated workers at his heels.

Soon all was quiet and orderly again in Paradise, S. C. On the advice of a conciliator from the United States Labor Department, Blickdoff and Hortzenboff took immediate steps to make their workers more satisfied with their pay, their jobs and their little home town. They built a swimming pool, a tennis court, shower baths and a playground for their employees but neglected to shorten their work time so these improvements could be enjoyed. They announced that they would give each worker a bonus of a whole day's pay at Christmas time hereafter, and a week's vacation each year to every employee who had been with them more than ten years. There were no such employees, of course, but the mill hands were overjoyed with their victory.

The local Baptist preacher, who was very thoughtfully paid by the company with the understanding that he would take a practical view of conditions in the community, told his flock their employers were to be commended for adopting a real Christian and American way of settling the difficulties between them and their workers. He suggested it was quite likely that Jesus, placed in the same position, would have done likewise.

"Be thankful for the little things," he mooed. "God works in mysterious ways his wonders to perform. Ye shall know the truth and the truth shall set ye free. The basis of all things is truth. Let us not be led astray by the poison from vipers' tongues. This is America and not Russia. Patrick Henry said 'Give me liberty or give me death' and the true, red-blooded, 100 per cent American citizen says the same thing today. But there are right ways and wrong ways to get liberty. Your employers have gone about it the right way. For what, after all, is liberty except the enjoyment of life; and have they not placed within your reach those things that bring happiness and recreation?

"Your employers are interested, just as all true Americans are interested, in the welfare of their fellow citizens, their fellow townsmen. Their hearts beat for you. They are always thinking of you. They are always planning ways to make conditions better for you. They are sincerely doing all in their power. They have very heavy responsibilities.

"So you must be patient. Rome wasn't built in a day. All things turn out well in time. Christ knows what he is doing and he will not permit his children to suffer.

"O, ye of little faith! Let not your hearts store up jealousy, hatred and animosity. Let not your minds be wooed by misunderstanding. Let us try to act and think as God would wish us to, and above all, let us, like those two kindly men yonder, practice Christian tolerance."

Despite this inspiring message, it was apparent to everyone that Paradise would never be the same again. Rumors continued to fill the air. People were always asking each other embarrassing questions about birth and blood. Fights became more frequent. Large numbers of the workers, being of Southern birth, were unable to disprove charges of possessing Negro ancestry, and so were forced to leave the vicinity. The mill hands kept so busy talking about Negro blood that no one thought of discussing wages and hours of labor.

In August, Messrs. Blickdoff and Hortzenboff, being in Atlanta on business, stopped by Matthew's office.

"Well, how's the strike?" asked the Grand Giraw.

"Dot strike!" echoed Blickdoff. "Ach Gott! Dot strike neffer come off. Vat you do, you razcal?"

"That's my secret," replied Matthew, a little proudly. "Every man to his trade, you know."

It had indeed become Matthew's trade and he was quite adept at it. What had happened at Paradise had also happened elsewhere. There were no rumors of strikes. The working people were far more interested in what they considered, or were told was, the larger issue of race. It did not matter that they had to send their children into the mills to augment the family wave; that they were always sickly and that their death rate was high. What mattered such little things when the very foundation of civilization, white supremacy, was threatened?

EIGHT

For over two years now had Black-No-More, Incorporated, been carrying on its self-appointed task of turning Negroes into Caucasians. The job was almost complete, except for the black folk in prisons, orphan asylums, insane asylums, homes for the aged, houses of correction and similar institutions. Those who had always maintained that it was impossible to get Negroes together for anything but a revival, a funeral or a frolic now had to admit that they had coöperated well in getting white. The poor had been helped by the well-to-do, brothers had helped sisters, children had assisted parents. There had been revived some of the same spirit of adventure prevalent in the days of the Underground Railroad. As a result, even in Mississippi, Negroes were quite rare. In the North the only Negroes to be seen were mulatto babies whose mothers, charmed by the beautiful color of their offspring, had defied convention and not turned them white. As there had never been more than two million Negroes in the North, the whitening process had been viewed indifferently by the masses because those who controlled the channels of opinion felt that the country was getting rid of a very vexatious problem at absolutely no cost; but not so in the South.

When one-third of the population of the erstwhile Confederacy had consisted of the much-maligned Sons of Ham, the blacks had really been of economic, social and psychological value to the section. Not only had they done the dirty

work and laid the foundation of its wealth, but they had
served as a convenient red herring for the upper classes when
the white proletariat grew restive under exploitation. The
presence of the Negro as an under class had also made of
Dixie a unique part of the United States. There, despite the
trend to industrialization, life was a little different, a little
pleasanter, a little softer. There was contrast and variety,
which was rare in a nation where standardization had pro-
gressed to such an extent that a traveler didn't know what
town he was in until someone informed him. The South had
always been identified with the Negro, and vice versa, and
its most pleasant memories treasured in song and story were
built around this pariah class.

The deep concern of the Southern Caucasians with chivalry, the protection of white womanhood, the exaggerated
development of race pride and the studied arrogance of even
the poorest half-starved white peon were all due to the presence of the black man. Booted and starved by their industrial
and agricultural feudal lords, the white masses derived their
only consolation and happiness from the fact that they were
the same color as their oppressors and consequently better
than the mudsill blacks.

The economic loss to the South by the ethnic migration
was considerable. Hundreds of wooden railroad coaches,
long since condemned as death traps in all other parts of the
country, had to be scrapped by the railroads when there were
no longer any Negroes to jim crow. Thousands of railroad
waiting rooms remained unused because, having been set
aside for the use of Negroes, they were generally too dingy
and unattractive for white folk or were no longer necessary.
Thousands of miles of streets located in the former Black
Belts, and thus without sewers or pavement, were having to
be improved at the insistent behest of the rapidly increased
white population, real and imitation. Real estate owners who
had never dreamed of making repairs on their tumble-down
property when it was occupied by the docile Negroes were

having to tear down, rebuild and alter to suit white tenants. Shacks and drygoods boxes that had once sufficed as schools for Negro children had now to be condemned and abandoned as unsuitable for occupation by white youth. Whereas thousands of school teachers had received thirty and forty dollars a month because of their Negro ancestry, the various cities and countries of the Southland were now forced to pay the standard salaries prevailing elsewhere.

Naturally taxes increased. Chambers of Commerce were now unable to send out attractive advertising to Northern business firms offering no or very low taxation as an inducement to them to move South nor were they able to offer as many cheap building sites. Only through the efforts of the Grand Exalted Giraw of the Knights of Nordica were they still able to point to their large reserves of docile, contented, Anglo-Saxon labor, and who knew how long that condition would last?

Consequently, the upper classes faced the future with some misgivings. As if being deprived of the pleasure of black mistresses were not enough, there was a feeling that there would shortly be widespread revolt against the existing medieval industrial conditions and resultant reduction of profits and dividends. The mill barons viewed with distaste the prospect of having to do away with child labor. Rearing back in their padded swivel chairs, they leaned fat jowls on well-manicured hands and mourned the passing of the halcyon days of yore.

If the South had lost its Negroes, however, it had certainly not lost its vote, and the political oligarchy that ruled the section was losing its old assurance and complacency. The Republicans had made inroads here and there in the 1934 Congressional elections. The situation politically was changing and if drastic steps were not immediately taken, the Republicans might carry the erstwhile Solid South, thus practically destroying the Democratic Party. Another Presidential election was less than two years off. There would have to be fast work to ward off disaster. Far-sighted people,

North and South, even foresaw the laboring people soon forsaking both of the old parties and going Socialist. Politicians and business men shuddered at the thought of such a tragedy and saw horrible visions of old-age pensions, eight-hour laws, unemployment insurance, workingmen's compensation, minimum-wage legislation, abolition of child labor, dissemination of birth-control information, monthly vacations for female workers, two-month vacations for prospective mothers, both with pay, and the probable killing of individual initiative and incentive by taking the ownership of national capital out of the hands of two million people and putting it into the hands of one hundred and twenty million.

Which explains why Senator Rufus Kretin of Georgia, one of the old Democratic war horses, an incomparable Negro-baiter, a faithful servitor of the dominant economic interests of his state and the lusty father of several black families since whitened, walked into the office of Imperial Grand Wizard Givens one day in March, 1935.

"Boys," he began, as closeted with Rev. Givens, Matthew and Bunny in the new modernistic Knights of Nordica palace, they quaffed cool and illegal beverages, "we gotta do sumpin and do it quick. These heah damn Yankees ah makin' inroads on ouah preserves, suh. Th' Republican vote is a-growin'. No tellin' what's li'ble tuh happen in this heah nex' 'lection."

"What can we do, Senator?" asked the Imperial Grand Wizard. "How can we serve the cause?"

"That's just it. That's just it, suh; jus' what Ah came heah fo'," replied the Senator. "Naow sum o' us was thinkin' that maybe yo'all might be able to he'p us keep these damn hicks in line. Yo'all are intelligent gent'men; you know what Ah'm gettin' at?"

"Well, that's a pretty big order, Colonel," said Givens.

"Yes," Matthew added. "It'll be a hard proposition. Conditions are no longer what they used to be."

"An'," said Givens, "we can't do much with that nigger business, like we used to do when th' old Klan was runnin'."

"What about one o' them theah Red scares?" asked the Senator, hopefully.

"Humph!" the clergyman snorted. "Better leave that there Red Business alone. Times ain't like they was, you know. Anyhow, them damn Reds'll be down here soon enough 'thout us encouragin' 'em none."

"Guess that's right, Gen'ral," mused the statesman. Then brightening: "Lookaheah, Givens. This fellah Fisher's gotta good head. Why not let him work out sumpin?"

"Yeah, he sure has," agreed the Wizard, glad to escape any work except minding the treasury of his order. "If he can't do it, ain't nobody can. Him and Bunny here is as shrewd as some o' them old time darkies. He! He! He!" He beamed patronizingly upon his brilliant son-in-law and his plump secretary.

"Well, theah's money in it. We got plenty o' cash; what we want now is votes," the Senator explained. "C'ose yuh caint preach that white supremacy stuff ve'y effectively when they haint no niggahs."

"Leave it to me. I'll work out something," said Matthew. Here was a chance to get more power, more money. Busy as he was, it would not do to let the opportunity slip by.

"Yuh caint lose no time," warned the Senator.

"We won't," crowed Givens.

A few minutes later they took a final drink together, shook hands and the Senator, bobbing his white head to the young ladies in the outer office, departed.

Matthew and Bunny retired to the private office of the Grand Exalted Giraw.

"What you thinkin' about pullin'?" asked Bunny.

"Plenty. We'll try the old sure fire Negro problem stuff."

"But that's ancient history, Brother," protested Bunny. "These ducks won't fall for that anymore."

"Bunny, I've learned something on this job, and that is

that hatred and prejudice always go over big. These people have been raised on the Negro problem, they're used to it, they're trained to react to it. Why should I rack my brain to hunt up something else when I can use a dodge that's always delivered the goods?"

"It may go over at that."

"I know it will. Just leave it to me," said Matthew confidently. "That's not worrying me at all. What's got my goat is my wife being in the family way." Matthew stopped bantering a moment, a sincere look of pain erasing his usual ironic expression.

"Congratulations!" burbled Bunny.

"Don't rub it in," Matthew replied. "You know how the kid will look."

"That's right," agreed his pal. "You know, sometimes I forget who we are."

"Well, I don't. I know I'm a darky and I'm always on the alert."

"What do you intend to do?"

"I don't know, Big Boy, I don't know. I would ordinarily send her to one of those lying-in hospitals but she'd be suspicious. Yet, if the kid is born it'll sure be black."

"It won't be white," Bunny agreed. "Why not tell her the whole thing and since she's so crazy about you, I don't think she'd hesitate to go."

"Man, you must be losing your mind, or else you've lost it!" Matthew exploded. "She's a worse nigger-hater than her father. She'd holler for a divorce before you could say Jack Robinson."

"You've got too much money for that."

"You're assuming that she has plenty of intelligence."

"Hasn't she?"

"Let's not discuss a painful subject," pleaded Matthew. "Suggest a remedy."

"She don't have to know that she's going to one of Crookman's places, does she?"

"No, but I can't get her to leave home to have the baby."

"Why?"

"Oh, a lot of damn sentiment about having her baby in the old home, and her damned old mother supports her. So what can I do?"

"Then, the dear old homestead is the only thing that's holding up the play?"

"You're a smart boy, Bunny."

"Don't stress the obvious. Seriously, though, I think everything can be fixed okeh."

"How?" cried Matthew, eagerly.

"Is it worth five grand?" countered Bunny.

"Money's no object, you know, but explain your proposition."

"I will not. You get me fifty century notes and I'll explain later."

"It's a deal, old friend."

Bunny Brown was a man of action. That evening he entered the popular Niggerhead Café, rendezvous of the questionable classes, and sat down at a table. The place was crowded with drinkers downing their "white mule" and contorting to the strains issuing from a radio loud speaker. A current popular dance piece, "The Black Man Blues," was filling the room. The songwriters had been making a fortune recently writing sentimental songs about the passing of the Negro. The plaintive voice of a blues singer rushed out of the loud-speaker:

> I wonder where my big, black man has gone;
> Oh, I wonder where my big, black man has gone.
> Has he done got faded an' left me all alone?

When the music ceased and the dancers returned to their tables, Bunny began to look around. In a far corner he saw a waiter whose face seemed familiar. He waited until the fellow came close when he hailed him. As the waiter bent over to get

his order, he studied him closely. He had seen this fellow somewhere before. Who could he be? Suddenly with a start he re-
membered. It was Dr. Joseph Bonds, former head of the Negro
Data League in New York. What had brought him here and
to this condition? The last time he had seen Bonds, the fellow
was a power in the Negro world, with a country place in West-
chester County and a swell apartment in town. It saddened
Bunny to think that catastrophe had overtaken such a man.
Even getting white, it seemed, hadn't helped him much. He
recalled that Bonds in his heyday had collected from the white
philanthropists with the slogan: "Work, Not Charity," and
he smiled as he thought that Bonds would be mighty glad now
to get a little charity and not so much work.

"Would a century note look good to you right now?" he
asked the former Negro leader when he returned with
his drink.

"Just show it to me, Mister," said the waiter, licking his
lips. "What you want me to do?"

"What will you do for a hundred berries?" pursued Bunny.

"I'd hate to tell you," replied Bonds, grinning and revealing his familiar tobacco-stained teeth.

"Have you got a friend you can trust?"

"Sure, a fellow named Licorice that washes pots in back."

"You don't mean Santop Licorice, do you?"

"Ssh! They don't know who he is here. He's white now,
you know."

"Do they know who you are?"

"What do you mean?" gasped the surprised waiter.

"Oh, I won't say anything but I know you're Bonds of
New York."

"Who told you?"

"Oh, a little fairy."

"How could that be? I never associate with them."

"It wasn't that kind of a fairy," Bunny reassured him,
laughing. "Well, you get Licorice and come to my hotel when
this place closes up."

"Where is that?" asked Bonds. Bunny wrote his name and room number down on a piece of paper and handed it to him.

Three hours later Bunny was awakened by a knocking at his door. He admitted Bonds and Licorice, the latter smelling strongly of steam and food.

"Here," said Bunny, holding up a hundred-dollar bill, "is a century note. If you boys can lay aside your scruples for a few hours you can have five of them apiece."

"Well," said Bonds, "neither Santop nor I have been over-burdened with them."

"That's what I thought," Bunny murmured. He proceeded to outline the work he wanted them to do.

"But that would be a criminal offense," objected Licorice.

"You too, Brutus?" sneered Bonds.

"Well, we can't afford to take chances unless we're pro-tected," the former President of Africa argued rather weakly. He was money-hungry and was longing for a stake to get back to Demerara where, since there was a large Negro pop-ulation, a white man, by virtue of his complexion, amounted to something. Yet he had had enough experience behind the bars to make him wary.

"We run this town and this state, too," Bunny assured him. "We could get a couple of our men to pull this stunt but it wouldn't be good policy."

"How about a thousand bucks apiece?" asked Bonds, his eyes glittering as he viewed the crisp banknotes in Bun-ny's hand.

"Here," said Bunny. "Take this century note between you, get your material and pull the job. When you've finished I'll give you nineteen more like it between you."

The two cronies looked at each other and nodded.

"It's a go," said Bonds.

They departed and Bunny went back to sleep.

The next night about eleven-thirty the bells began to toll and the mournful sirens of the fire engines awakened the entire neighborhood in the vicinity of Rev. Givens's home. That stately edifice, built by Ku Klux Klan dollars, was in flames. Firemen played a score of streams onto the blaze but the house appeared to be doomed.

On a lawn across the street, in the midst of a consoling crowd, stood Rev. and Mrs. Givens, Helen and Matthew. The old couple were taking the catastrophe fatalistically, Matthew was puzzled and suspicious, but Helen was in hysterics. She presented a bedraggled and woebegone appearance with a blanket around her night dress. She wept afresh every time she looked across at the blazing building where she had spent her happy childhood.

"Matthew," she sobbed, "will you build me another one just like it?"

"Why certainly, Honey," he agreed, "but it will take quite a while."

"Oh, I know; I know, but I want it."

"Well, you'll get it, darling," he soothed, "but I think it would be a good idea for you to go away for a while to rest your nerves. We've got to think of the little one that's coming, you know."

"I don't wanna go nowhere," she screamed.

"But you've got to go somewhere," he reasoned. "Don't you think so, Mother?" Old Mrs. Givens agreed it would be a good idea but suggested that she go along. To this Rev. Givens would not listen at first but he finally yielded.

"Guess it's a good idea after all," he remarked. "Women folks is always in th' way when buildin's goin' on."

Matthew was tickled at the turn of affairs. On the way down to the hotel, he sat beside Helen, alternately comforting her and wondering as to the origin of the fire.

Next morning, bright and early, Bunny, grinning broadly, walked into the office, threw his hat on a hook and sat down before his desk after the customary salutation.

"Bunny," called Matthew, looking at him hard. "Get me told!"

"What do you mean?" asked Bunny innocently.

"Just as I thought," chuckled Matthew. "You're a nervy guy."

"Why, I don't get you," said Bunny, continuing the pose.

"Come clean, Big Boy. How much did that fire cost?"

"You gave me five grand, didn't you?"

"Just like a nigger: a person can never get a direct answer from you."

"Are you satisfied?"

"I'm not crying my eyes out."

"Is Helen going North for her confinement?"

"Nothing different."

"Well, then, why do you want to know the why and wherefore of that blaze?"

"Just curiosity, Nero, old chap," grinned Matthew.

"Remember," warned Bunny, mischievously, "curiosity killed the cat."

The ringing of the telephone bell interrupted their conversation.

"What's that?" yelled Matthew into the mouthpiece. "The hell you say! All right, I'll be right up." He hung up the receiver, jumped up excitedly and grabbed his hat.

"What's the matter?" shouted Bunny. "Somebody dead?"

"No," answered the agitated Matthew, "Helen's had a miscarriage," and he dashed out of the room.

"Somebody dead right on," murmured Bunny, half aloud.

Joseph Bonds and Santop Licorice, clean-shaven and immaculate, followed the Irish red cap into their drawing room on the New York Express.

"It sure feels good to get out of the barrel once more," sighed Bonds, dropping down on the soft cushion and pulling out a huge cigar.

"Ain't it the truth?" agreed the former Admiral of the Royal African Navy.

NINE

Bunny, I've got it all worked out," announced Matthew, several mornings later, as he breezed into the office.

"Got what worked out?"

"The political proposition."

"Spill it."

"Well, here it is: First, we get Givens on the radio; national hookup, you know, once a week for about two months."

"What'll he talk about? Are you going to write it for him?"

"Oh, he knows how to charm the yokels. He'll appeal to the American people to call upon the Republican administration to close up the sanitariums of Dr. Crookman and deport everybody connected with Black-No-More."

"You can't deport citizens, silly," Bunny remonstrated.

"That don't stop you from advocating it. This is politics, Big Boy."

"Well, what else is on the program?"

"Next: We start a campaign of denunciation against the Republicans in *The Warning*, connecting them with the Pope, Black-No-More and anything else we can think of."

"But they were practically anti-Catholic in 1928, weren't they?"

"Seven years ago, Bunny, seven years ago. How often must I tell you that the people never remember anything? Next we pull the old Write-to-your-Congressman-Write-to-your-Senator stuff. We carry the form letter in *The Warning*, the readers do the rest."

"You can't win a campaign on that stuff alone," said Bunny disdainfully. "Bring me something better than that, Brother."

"Well, the other step is a surprise, old chap. I'm going to keep it under my hat until later on. But when I spring it, old time, it'll knock everybody for a row of toadstools." Matthew smiled mysteriously and smoothed back his pale blond hair.

"When do we start this radio racket?" yawned Bunny.

"Wait'll I talk it over with the Chief," said Matthew, rising, "and see how he's dated up."

The following Thursday evening at 8:15 P.M. millions of people sat before their loud speakers, expectantly awaiting the heralded address to the nation by the Imperial Grand Wizard of the Knights of Nordica. The program started promptly:

"Good evening, ladies and gentlemen of the radio audience. This is Station WHAT, Atlanta, Ga., Mortimer K. Shanker announcing. This evening we are offering a program of tremendous interest to every American citizen. The countrywide hookup over the chain of the Moronia Broadcasting Company is enabling one hundred million citizens to hear one of the most significant messages ever delivered to the American public.

"Before introducing the distinguished speaker of the evening, however, I have a little treat in store for you. Mr. Jack Albert, the well-known Broadway singer and comedian, has kindly consented to render his favorite among the popular songs of the day, 'Vanishing Mammy.' Mr. Albert will be accompanied by that incomparable aggregation of musical talent, Sammy Snort's Bogalusa Babies. . . . Come on, Al, say a word or two to the ladies and gentlemen of the radio audience before you begin."

"Oh, hello folks. Awfully glad to see so many of you out there tonight. Well, that is to say, I suppose there are many of you out there. You know I like to flatter myself, besides I haven't my glasses so I can't see very well. However, that's not the pint, as the bootleggers say. I'm terribly pleased to have the opportunity of starting off a program like this with one of the songs I have come to love best. You know, I think a whole lot of this song. I like it because it has feeling and sentiment. It means something. It carries you back to the good old days that are dead and gone forever. It was written by Johnny Gulp with music by the eminent Japanese-American composer Forkrise Sake. And, as Mr. Shanker told you, I am being accompanied by Sammy Snort's Bogalusa Babies through the courtesy of the Artillery Café, Chicago, Illinois. All right, Sammy, smack it!"

In two seconds the blare of the jazz orchestra smote the ears of the unseen audience with the weird medley and clash of sound that had passed for music since the days of the Panama-Pacific Exposition. Then the sound died to a whisper and the plaintive voice of America's premier black-faced troubadour came over the air:

> Vanishing Mammy, Mammy! Mammy! of Mi—ne,
> You've been away, dear, such an awfully long time
> You went away, Sweet Mammy! Mammy! one summer night
> I can't help thinkin', Mammy, that you went white.
> Of course I can't blame you, Mammy! Mammy! dear
> Because you had so many troubles, Mammy, to bear.
> But the old homestead hasn't been the same
> Since I last heard you, Mammy, call my name.
> And so I wait, loving Mammy, it seems in vain,
> For you to come waddling back home again
> Vanishing Mammy! Mammy! Mammy!
> I'm waiting for you to come back home again.

"Now, radio audience, this is Mr. Mortimer Shanker speaking again. I know you all loved Mr. Albert's soulful rendition of 'Vanishing Mammy.' We're going to try to get him back again in the very near future.

"It now gives me great pleasure to introduce to you a man who hardly needs any introduction. A man who is known throughout the civilized world. A man of great scholarship, executive ability and organizing genius. A man who has, practically unassisted, brought five million Americans under the banner of one of the greatest societies in this country. It affords me great pleasure, ladies and gentlemen of the radio audience, to introduce Rev. Henry Givens, Imperial Grand Wizard of the Knights of Nordica, who will address you on the very timely topic of 'The Menace of Negro Blood.'"

Rev. Givens, fortified with a slug of corn, advanced nervously to the microphone, fingering his prepared address. He cleared his throat and talked for upwards of an hour during which time he successfully[avoided saying anything that was true,]the result being that thousands of telegrams and long-distance telephone calls of congratulation came in to the studio. In his long address he discussed the foundations of the Republic, anthropology, psychology, miscegenation, coöperation with Christ, getting right with God, curbing Bolshevism, the bane of birth control, the menace of the Modernists, science versus religion, and many other subjects of which he was[totally ignorant.]The greater part of his time was taken up in a denunciation of Black-No-More, Incorporated, and calling upon the Republican administration of President Harold Goosie to deport the vicious Negroes at the head of it or imprison them in the federal penitentiary. When he had concluded "In the name of our Savior and Redeemer, Jesus Christ, Amen," he retired hastily to the washroom to finish his half-pint of corn.

The announcer took Rev. Givens's place at the microphone:

"Now friends, this is Mortimer K. Shanker again, announcing from Station WHAT, Atlanta, Ga., with a nationwide hookup over the chain of the Moronia Broadcasting Company. You have just heard a scholarly and inspiring address by Rev. Henry Givens, Imperial Grand Wizard of the Knights of Nordica on 'The Menace of Negro Blood.' Rev.

Givens will deliver another address at this station a week from tonight. . . . Now, to end our program for the evening, friends, we are going to have a popular song by the well-known Goyter Sisters, lately of the State Street Follies, entitled 'Why Did the Old Salt Shaker'. . . ."

The agitation of the Knights of Nordica soon brought action from the administration at Washington. About ten days after Rev. Givens had ceased his talks over the radio, President Harold Goosie announced to the assembled newspaper men that he was giving a great deal of study to the questions raised by the Imperial Grand Wizard concerning Black-No-More, Incorporated; that several truckloads of letters condemning the corporation had been received at the White House and were now being answered by a special corps of clerks; that several Senators had talked over the matter with him, and that the country could expect him to take some action within the next fortnight.

At the end of a fortnight, the President announced that he had decided to appoint a commission of leading citizens to study the whole question thoroughly and to make recommendations. He asked Congress for an appropriation of $100,000 to cover the expenses of the commission.

The House of Representatives approved a resolution to that effect a week later. The Senate, which was then engaged in a spirited debate on the World Court and the League of Nations, postponed consideration of the resolution for three weeks. When it came to vote before that august body, it was passed, after long argument, with amendments and returned to the House.

Six weeks after President Goosie had made his request of Congress, the resolution was passed in its final form. He then announced that inside of a week he would name the members of the commission.

The President kept his word. He named the commission, consisting of seven members, five Republicans and two

Democrats. They were mostly politicians temporarily out of a job.

In a private car the commission toured the entire country, visiting all of the Black-No-More sanitariums, the Crookman lying-in hospitals and the former Black Belts. They took hundreds of depositions, examined hundreds of witnesses and drank large quantities of liquor.

Two months later they issued a preliminary report in which they pointed out that the Black-No-More sanitariums and lying-in hospitals were being operated within the law; that only one million Negroes remained in the country; that it was illegal in most of the states for pure whites and persons of Negro ancestry to intermarry but that it was difficult to detect fraud because of collusion. As a remedy the commission recommended stricter observance of the law, minor changes in the marriage laws, the organization of special matrimonial courts with trained genealogists attached to each, better equipped judges, more competent district attorneys, the strengthening of the Mann Act, the abolition of the road house, the closer supervision of dance halls, a stricter censorship on books and moving pictures and government control of cabarets. The commission promised to publish the complete report of its activities in about six weeks.

Two months later, when practically everyone had forgotten that there had ever been such an investigation, the complete report of the commission, comprising 1,789 pages in fine print, came off the press. Copies were sent broadcast to prominent citizens and organizations. Exactly nine people in the United States read it: the warden of a country jail, the proofreader at the Government Printing Office, the janitor of the City Hall in Ashtabula, Ohio, the city editor of the Helena (Ark.) *Bugle*, a stenographer in the Department of Health of Spokane, Wash., a dishwasher in a Bowery restaurant, a flunky in the office of the Research Director of Black-No-More, Incorporated, a life termer in Clinton Prison at Dannemora, N. Y., and a gag writer on the staff of a humorous weekly in Chicago.

Matthew received fulsome praise from the members of his organization and the higher-ups in the Southern Democracy. He had, they said, forced the government to take action, and they began to[talk of him for public office.]

The Grand Exalted Giraw was jubilant. Everything, he told Bunny, had gone as he had planned. Now he was ready to turn the next trick.

"What's that?" asked his assistant, looking up from the morning comic section.

"Ever hear of the Anglo-Saxon Association of America?" Matthew queried.

"No, what's their graft?"

"It isn't a graft, you crook. The Anglo-Saxon Association of America is an organization located in Virginia. The headquarters are in Richmond. It's a group of rich highbrows who can trace their ancestry back almost two hundred years. You see they believe in white supremacy the same as our outfit but they claim that the Anglo-Saxons are the cream of the white race and should maintain the leadership in American social, economic and political life."

"You sound like a college professor," sneered Bunny.

"Don't insult me, you tripe. Listen now: This crowd thinks they're too highbrow to come in with the Knights of Nordica. They say our bunch are morons."

"That about makes it unanimous," commented Bunny, biting off the end of a cigar. intricate

"Well, what I'm trying to do now is to bring these two organizations together. We've got numbers but not enough money to win an election; they have the jack. If I can get them to see the light we'll win the next Presidential election hands down."

"What'll I be: Secretary of the Treasury?" laughed Bunny.

"Over my dead body!" Matthew replied, reaching for his

flask. "But seriously, Old Top, if I can succeed in putting this deal over we'll have the White House in a bag. No fooling!"

"When do we get busy?"

"Next week this Anglo-Saxon Association has its annual meeting in Richmond. You and I'll go up there and give them a spiel. We may take Givens along to add weight."

"You don't mean intellectual weight, do you?"

"Will you never stop kidding?"

Mr. Arthur Snobbcraft, President of the Anglo-Saxon Association, an F. F. V. and a man suspiciously swarthy for an Anglo-Saxon, had devoted his entire life to fighting for two things: white racial integrity and Anglo-Saxon supremacy. It had been very largely a losing fight. The farther he got from his goal, the more desperate he became. He had been the genius that thought up the numerous racial integrity laws adopted in Virginia and many of the other Southern states. He was strong for sterilization of the unfit: meaning Negroes, aliens, Jews and other riff raff, and he had an abiding hatred of democracy.

Snobbcraft's pet scheme now was to get a genealogical law passed disfranchising all people of Negro or unknown ancestry. He argued that good citizens could not be made out of such material. His organization had money but it needed popularity—numbers.

His joy then knew no bounds when he received Matthew's communication. While he had no love for the Knights of Nordica which, he held, contained just the sort of people he wanted to legislate into impotency, social, economic and physical, he believed he could use them to gain his point. He wired Matthew at once, saying the Association would be delighted to have him address them, as well as the Imperial Grand Wizard.

The Grand Exalted Giraw had long known of Snobbcraft's obsession, the genealogical law. He also knew that there was no chance of ever getting such a law adopted but in order to even try to pass such a law it would be necessary to win the whole country in a national election. Together, his organization and Snobbcraft's could turn the trick; singly neither one could do it.

In an old pre–Civil War mansion on a broad, tree-shaded boulevard, the directors of the Anglo-Saxon Association gathered in their annual meeting. They listened first to Rev. Givens and next to Matthew. The matter was referred to a committee which in an hour or two reported favorably. Most of these men had dreamed from youth of holding high political office at the national capital as had so many eminent Virginians but none of them was Republican, of course, and the Democrats never won anything nationally. By swallowing their pride for a season and joining with the riff raff of the Knights of Nordica, they saw an opportunity, for the first time in years to get into power; and they took it. They would furnish plenty of money, they said, if the other group would furnish the numbers.

Givens and Matthew returned to Atlanta in high spirits.

"I tell you, Brother Fisher," croaked Givens, "our star is ascending. I can see no way for us to fail, with God's help. We'll surely defeat our enemy. Victory is in the air."

"It sure looks that way," the Grand Giraw agreed. "With their money and ours, we can certainly get together a larger campaign fund than the Republicans."

Back in Richmond Mr. Snobbcraft and his friends were in conference with the statistician of a great New York insurance company. This man, Dr. Samuel Buggerie, was highly respected among members of his profession and well known by the reading public. He was the author of several books and wrote frequently for the heavier periodicals. His well-known work, *The Fluctuation of the Sizes of Left Feet among the Assyrians during the Ninth Century before Christ*, had been favorably commented upon by several reviewers, one of whom had actually read it. An even more learned work of his was entitled *Putting Wasted Energy to Work*, in which he called attention, by elaborate charts and graphs, to the possibilities of harnessing the power generated by the leaves of trees rubbing together on windy days. In several brilliant monographs he had proved that rich people have smaller families than the poor; that imprisonment does not stop crime; that laborers usually migrate in the wake of high wages. In his most recent article in a very intellectual magazine read largely by those who loafed for a living, he had proved statistically that unemployment and poverty are principally a state of mind. This contribution was enthusiastically hailed by scholars and especially by business men as an outstanding contribution to contemporary thought.

Dr. Buggerie was a ponderous, nervous, entirely bald specimen of humanity, with thick moist hands, a receding double chin and very prominent eyes that were constantly shifting about and bearing an expression of seemingly perpetual wonderment behind their big horn-rimmed spectacles. He seemed about to burst out of his clothes and his pockets were always bulging with papers and notes.

Dr. Buggerie, like Mr. Snobbcraft, was a professional Anglo-Saxon as well as a descendant of one of the First Families of Virginia. He held that the only way to tell the pure whites from the imitation whites was to study their family trees. He claimed that such a nationwide investigation would disclose the various non-Nordic strains in the population. Laws, said he, should then be passed forbidding these strains from mixing or marrying with the pure strains that had produced such fine specimens of mankind as Mr. Snobbcraft and himself.

In high falsetto voice he eagerly related to the directors of the Anglo-Saxon Association the results of some of his preliminary researches. These tended to show, he claimed, that there must be as many as twenty million people in the United States who possessed some slight non-Nordic strain and were thus unfit for both citizenship and procreation. If the organization would put up the money for the research on a national scale, he declared that he could produce statistics before election that would be so shocking that the Republicans would lose the country unless they adopted the Democratic plank on genealogical examinations. After a long and eloquent talk by Mr. Snobbcraft in support of Dr. Buggerie's proposition, the directors voted to appropriate the money, on condition that the work be kept as secret as possible. The statistician agreed although it hurt him to the heart to forego any publicity. The very next morning he began quietly to assemble his staff.

TEN

Hank Johnson, Chuck Foster, Dr. Crookman and Gorman Gay, National Chairman of the Republican National Committee, sat in the physician's hotel suite conversing in low tones.

"We're having a tough time getting ready for the fall campaign," said Gay. "Unfortunately our friends are not contributing with their accustomed liberality."

"Can't complain about us, can you?" asked Foster.

"No, no," the politician denied quickly. "You have been most liberal in the past two years, but then we have done many favors for you, too."

"Yuh sho right, Gay," Hank remarked. "Dem crackahs mighta put us outa business efen it hadn' bin fo' the' admin'strations suppo't."

"I'm quite sure we deeply appreciate the many favors we've received from the present administration," added Dr. Crookman.

"We won't need it much longer, though," said Chuck Foster.

"How's that?" asked Gay, opening his half-closed eyes.

"Well, we've done about all the business we can do in this country. Practically all of the Negroes are white except a couple of thousand diehards and those in institutions," Chuck informed him.

"Dat's right," said Hank. "An' it sho makes dis heah country lonesome. Ah ain't seen a brownskin ooman in so long Ah doan know what Ah'd do if Ah seen one."

"That's right, Gay," added Dr. Crookman. ["We've about cleaned up the Negro problem in this country.] Next week we're closing all except five of our sanitariums."

"Well, what about your lying-in hospitals?" asked Gay.

"Of course we'll have to continue operating them," Crookman replied. "The women would be in an awful fix if we didn't."

"Now look here," proposed Gay, drawing closer to them and lowering his voice. "This coming campaign is going to be one of the bitterest in the history of this country. I fear there will be rioting, shooting and killing. Those hospitals cannot be closed without tremendous mental suffering to the womanhood of the country. We want to avoid that and you want to avoid it, too. Yet, these hospitals will constantly be in danger. It ought to be worth something to you to have them especially protected by the forces of the government."

"You would do that anyway, wouldn't you Gay?" asked Crookman.

"Well, it's going to cost us millions of votes to do it, and the members of the National Executive Committee seem to feel that you ought to make a very liberal donation to the campaign fund to make up for the votes we'll lose."

"What would you call a liberal donation?" Crookman inquired.

"A successful campaign cannot be fought this year," Gay replied, "under twenty millions."

"Man," shouted Hank, "yuh ain't talkin' 'bout dollahs, is yuh?"

"You got it right, Hank," answered the National Chairman. "It'll cost that much and maybe more."

"Where do you expect to get all of that money?" queried Foster.

"That's just what's worrying us," Gay replied, "and that's why I'm here. You fellows are rolling in wealth and we need your help. In the past two years you've collected around ninety million dollars from the Negro public. Why not give us a good break? You won't miss five million, and it ought to be worth it to you fellows to defeat the Democrats."

"Five millions! Great Day," Hank exploded. "Man, is you los' yo' min'?"

"Not at all," Gay denied. "Might as well own up that if we don't get a contribution of about that size from you we're liable to lose this election. . . . Come on, fellows, don't be so tight. Of course, you're setting pretty and all you've got to do is change your residence to Europe or some other place if things don't run smoothly in America, but you want to think of those poor women with their black babies. What will they do if you fellows leave the country or if the Democrats win and you have to close all of your places?"

"That's right, Chief," Foster observed. "You can't let the women down."

"Yeah," said Johnson. "Give 'im the jack."

"Well, suppose we do?" concluded Crookman, smiling.

The National Chairman was delighted. "When can we collect?" he asked, "and how?"

"Tomorrow, if yuh really wants it then," Johnson observed.

"Now remember," warned Gay. "We cannot afford to let it be known that we are getting such a large sum from any one person or corporation."

"That's your lookout," said the physician, indifferently. "You know *we* won't say anything."

Mr. Gay, shortly afterward, departed to carry the happy news to the National Executive Committee, then in session right there in New York City.

The Republicans certainly needed plenty of money to re-elect President Goosie. The frequent radio addresses of Rev. Givens, the growing numbers of the Knights of Nordica, the inexplicable affluence of the Democratic Party and the vitriolic articles in *The Warning* had not failed to rouse much Democratic sentiment. People were not exactly for the Democrats but they were against the Republicans. As early as

May it did not seem possible for the Republicans to carry a single Southern state and many of the Northern and Eastern strongholds were in doubt. The Democrats seemed to have everything their way. Indeed, they were so confident of success that they were already counting the spoils.

When the Democratic Convention met in Jackson, Mississippi, on July 1, 1936, political wiseacres claimed that for the first time in history the whole program was cut and dried and would be run off smoothly and swiftly. Such, however, was not the case. The unusually hot sun, coupled with the enormous quantities of liquor vended, besides the many conflicting interests present, soon brought dissension.

Shortly after the keynote speech had been delivered by Senator Kretin, the Anglo-Saxon crowd let it be known that they wanted some distinguished Southerner like Arthur Snobbcraft nominated for the Presidency. The Knights of Nordica were intent on nominating Imperial Grand Wizard Givens. The Northern faction of the party, now reduced to a small minority in party councils, was holding out for former Governor Grogan of Massachusetts, who as head of the League of Catholic Voters had a great following.

Through twenty ballots the voting proceeded, and it remained deadlocked. No faction would yield. Leaders saw that there had to be a compromise. They retired to a suite on the top floor of the Judge Lynch Hotel. There, in their shirt sleeves, with collars open, mint juleps on the table and electric fans stirring up the hot air, they got down to business. Twelve hours later they were still there.

Matthew, wilted, worn but determined, fought for his chief. Simeon Dump of the Anglo-Saxon Association swore he would not withdraw the name of Arthur Snobbcraft. Rev. John Whiffle, a power in the party, gulped drink after drink, kept dabbing a damp handkerchief at the shining surface of his skull, and held out for one Bishop Belch. Moses Lejewski of New York argued obstinately for the nomination of Governor Grogan.

In the meantime the delegates, having left the ovenlike convention hall, either lay panting and drinking in their rooms, sat in the hotel lobbies discussing the deadlock or cruised the streets in automobiles confidently seeking the dens of iniquity which they had been told were eager to lure them into sin.

When the clock struck three, Matthew rose and suggested that since the Knights of Nordica and the Anglo-Saxon Association were the two most powerful organizations in the party, Givens should get the Presidential nomination, Snobbcraft the Vice-Presidential and the other candidates be assured of cabinet positions. This suggested compromise appealed to no one except Matthew.

"You people forget," said Simeon Dump, "that the Anglo-Saxon Association is putting up half the money to finance this campaign."

"And you forget," declared Moses Lejewski, "that we're supporting your crazy scheme to disfranchise anybody possessing Negro ancestry when we get into office. That's going to cost us millions of votes in the North. You fellows can't expect to hog everything."

"Why not?" challenged Dump. "How could you win without money?"

"And how," added Matthew, "can you get anywhere without the Knights of Nordica behind you?"

"And how," Rev. Whiffle chimed in, "can you get anywhere without the Fundamentalists and the Drys?"

At four o'clock they had got no farther than they had been at three. They tried to pick some one not before mentioned, and went over and over the list of eligibles. None was satisfactory. One was too radical, another was too conservative, a third was an atheist, a fourth had once rifled a city treasury, the fifth was of immigrant extraction once removed, a sixth had married a Jewess, a seventh was an intellectual, an eighth had spent too long at Hot Springs trying to cure the syphilis, a ninth was rumored to be part Mexican and a tenth had at one time in his early youth been a Socialist.

At five o'clock they were desperate, drunk and disgusted. The stuffy room was a litter of discarded collars, cigarette and cigar butts, match stems, heaped ash trays and empty bottles. Matthew drank little and kept insisting on the selection of Rev. Givens. To the sodden and nodding men he painted marvelous pictures of the spoils of office and their excellent chance of getting there, and then suddenly declared that the Knights of Nordica would withdraw unless Givens was nominated. The threat aroused them. They cursed and called it a holdup, but Matthew was adamant. At a last stroke, he rose and pretended to be ready to bolt the caucus. They remonstrated with him and finally gave in to him.

Orders went out to the delegates. They assembled in the convention hall. The shepherds of the various state flocks cracked the whip and the delegates voted accordingly. Late that afternoon the news went out to a waiting world that the Democrats had nominated Henry Givens for President and Arthur Snobbcraft for Vice-President. Mr. Snobbcraft didn't like that at all, but it was better than nothing.

A few days later the Republican convention opened in Chicago. Better disciplined, as usual, than the Democrats, its business proceeded like clockwork. President Goosie was nominated for reëlection on the first ballot and Vice-President Gump was again selected as his running mate. A platform was adopted whose chief characteristic was vagueness. As was customary, it stressed the party's record in office, except that which was criminal; it denounced fanaticism without being specific, and it emphasized the rights of the individual and the trusts in the same paragraph. As the Democratic slogan was White Supremacy and its platform dwelt largely on the necessity of genealogical investigation, the Republicans adopted the slogan: Personal Liberty and Ancestral Sanctity.

Dr. Crookman and his associates, listening in on the radio in his suite in the Robin Hood Hotel in New York City, laughed softly as they heard the President deliver his speech of acceptance which ended in the following original manner:

"And finally, my friends, I can only say that we shall continue in the path of rugged individualism, free from the influence of sinister interests, upholding the finest ideals of honesty, independence and integrity, so that, to quote Abraham Lincoln, 'This nation of the people, for the people and by the people shall not perish from the earth.'"

"That," said Foster, as the President ceased barking, "sounds almost like the speech of acceptance of Brother Givens that we heard the other day."

Dr. Crookman smiled and brushed the ashes off his cigar. "It may even be the same speech," he suggested.

Through the hot days of July and August the campaign slowly got under way. Innumerable photographs appeared in the newspapers depicting the rival candidates among the simple folk of some village, helping youngsters to pick cherries, assisting an old woman up a stairway, bathing in the old swimming hole, eating at a barbecue and posing on the rear platforms of special trains.

Long articles appeared in the Sunday newspapers extolling the simple virtues of the two great men. Both, it seemed, had come from poor but honest families; both were hailed as tried and true friends of the great, common people; both were declared to be ready to give their strength and intellect to America for the next four years. One writer suggested that Givens resembled Lincoln, while another declared that President Goosie's character was not unlike that of Roosevelt, believing he was paying the former a compliment.

Rev. Givens told the reporters: "It is my intention, if elected, to carry out the traditional tariff policy of the Democratic Party" (neither he or anyone else knew what that was).

President Goosie averred again and again, "I intend to make my second term as honest and efficient as my first."

Though a dire threat, this statement was supposed to be a fine promise.

Meanwhile, Dr. Samuel Buggerie and his operatives were making great headway examining birth and marriage records throughout the United States. Around the middle of September the Board of Directors held a conference at which the learned man presented a partial report.

"I am now prepared to prove," gloated the obese statistician, "that fully one-quarter of the people of one Virginia county possess non-white ancestry, Indian or Negro; and we can further prove that all of the Indians on the Atlantic Coast are part Negro. In several counties in widely separated parts of the country, we have found that the ancestry of a considerable percentage of the people is in doubt. There is reason to believe that there are countless numbers of people who ought not to be classed with whites and should not mix with Anglo-Saxons."

It was decided that the statistician should get his data in simple form that anyone could read and understand, and have it ready to release just a few days before election. When the people saw how great was the danger from black blood, it was reasoned, they would flock to the Democratic standard and it would be too late for the Republicans to halt the stampede.

No political campaign in the history of the country had ever been so bitter. On one side were those who were fanatically positive of their pure Caucasian ancestry; on the other side were those who knew themselves to be "impure" white or had reason to suspect it. The former were principally Democratic, the latter Republican. There was another group which was Republican because it felt that a victory for the Democrats might cause another Civil War. The campaign roused acrimonious dispute even within families. Often behind these family rifts lurked the knowledge or suspicion of a dark past.

As the campaign grew more bitter, denunciations of Dr. Crookman and his activities grew more violent. A move was started to close all of his hospitals. Some wanted them to be closed for all time; others advised their closing for the duration of the campaign. The majority of thinking people (which wasn't so many) strenuously objected to the proposal.

"No good purpose will be served by closing these hospitals," declared the New York *Morning Earth*. "On the contrary such a step might have tragic results. The Negroes have disappeared into the body of our citizenry, large numbers have intermarried with the whites and the offspring of these marriages are appearing in increasing numbers. Without these hospitals, think how many couples would be estranged; how many homes wrecked! Instead of taking precipitate action, we should be patient and move slowly."

Other Northern newspapers assumed an even more friendly attitude, but the press generally followed the crowd, or led it, and in slightly veiled language urged the opponents of Black-No-More to take the law into their hands.

Finally, emboldened and inflamed by fiery editorials, radio addresses, pamphlets, posters and platform speeches, a mob seeking to protect white womanhood in Cincinnati attacked a Crookman hospital, drove several women into the streets and set fire to the building. A dozen babies were burned to death and others, hastily removed by their mothers, were recognized as mulattoes. The newspapers published names and addresses. Many of the women were very prominent socially either in their own right or because of their husbands.

The nation was shocked as never before. Republican sentiment began to dwindle. The Republican Executive Committee met and discussed ways and means of combating the trend. Gorman Gay was at his wits' end. Nothing, he thought, could save them except a miracle.

Two flights below in a spacious office sat two of the Republican campaigners, Walter Williams and Joseph Bonds,

busily engaged in leading the other workers (who knew better) to believe that they were earning the ten dollars a day
they were receiving. The former had passed for a Negro for
years on the strength of a part-Negro grandparent and then
gone back to the white race when the National Social Equality League was forced to cease operations at the insistence
of both the sheriff and the landlord. Joseph Bonds, former
head of the Negro Data League who had once been a Negro
but thanks to Dr. Crookman was now Caucasian and proud
of it, had but recently returned to the North from Atlanta,
accompanied by Santop Licorice. Both Mr. Williams and
Mr. Bonds had been unable to stomach the Democratic
crowd and so had fallen in with the Republicans, who were
as different from them as one billiard ball from another. The
two gentlemen were in low tones discussing the dilemma of
the Republicans, while rustling papers to appear busy.

"Jo, if we could figure out something to turn the tables on
these Democrats, we wouldn't have to work for the rest of
our lives," Williams observed, blowing a cloud of cigarette
smoke out of the other corner of his mouth.

"Yes, that's right, Walt, but there ain't a chance in the
world. Old Gay is almost crazy, you know. Came in here
slamming doors and snapping at everybody this morning,"
Bonds remarked.

Williams leaned closer to him, lowered his flame-thatched
head and then looking to the right and left whispered, "Listen here, do you know where Beard is?"

"No," answered Bonds, starting and looking around to
see if anyone was listening. "Where is he?"

"Well, I got a letter from him the other day. He's down
there in Richmond doing research work for the Anglo-Saxon
Association under that Dr. Buggerie."

"Do they know who he is?"

"Of course they don't. He's been white quite a while now,
you know, and of course they'd never connect him with the

Dr. Shakespeare A. Beard who used to be one of their most outspoken enemies."

"Well, what about it?" persisted Bonds, eagerly. "Do you think he might know something on the Democrats that might help?"

"He might. We could try him out anyway. If he knows anything he'll spill it because he hates that crowd."

"How will you get in touch with him quickly? Write to him?"

"Certainly not," growled Williams. "I'll get expenses from Gay for the trip. He'll fall for anything now."

He rose and made for the elevator. Five minutes later he was standing before his boss, the National Chairman, a worried, gray little man with an aldermaniac paunch and a convict's mouth.

"What is it, Williams?" snapped the Chairman.

"I'd like to get expenses to Richmond," said Williams. "I have a friend down there in Snobbcraft's office and he might have some dope we can use to our advantage."

"Scandal?" asked Mr. Gay, brightening.

"Well, I don't know right now, of course, but this fellow is a very shrewd observer and in six months' time he ought to have grabbed something that'll help us out of this jam."

"Is he a Republican or a Democrat?"

"Neither. He's a highly trained and competent social student. You couldn't expect him to be either," Williams observed. "But I happen to know that he hasn't got any money to speak of, so for a consideration I'm sure he'll spill everything he knows, if anything."

"Well, it's a gamble," said Gay, doubtfully, "but any port in a storm."

Williams left Washington immediately for Richmond. That night he sat in a cramped little room of the former champion of the darker races.

"What are you doing down there, Beard?" asked Williams,

referring to the headquarters of the Anglo-Saxon Association.

"Oh, I'm getting, or helping to get, that data of Buggerie's into shape."

"What data? You told me you were doing research work. Now you say you're arranging data. Have they finished collecting it?"

"Yes, we finished that job some time ago. Now we're trying to get the material in shape for easy digestion."

"What do you mean: easy digestion?" queried Williams. "What are you fellows trying to find out and why must it be so easily digested. You fellows usually try to make your stuff unintelligible to the herd."

"This is different," said Beard, lowering his voice to almost a whisper. "We're under a pledge of secrecy. We have been investigating the family trees of the nation and so far, believe me, we certainly have uncovered astounding facts. When I'm finally discharged, which will probably be after election, I'm going to peddle some of that information. Snobbcraft and even Buggerie are not aware of the inflammatory character of the facts we've assembled." He narrowed his foxy eyes greedily.

"Is it because they've been planning to release some of that they want it in easily digestible form, as you say?" pressed Williams.

"That's it exactly," declared Beard, stroking his now clean-shaven face. "I overheard Buggerie and Snobbcraft chuckling about it only a day or two ago."

"Well, there must be a whole lot of it," insinuated Williams, "if they've had all of you fellows working for six months. Where all did you work?"

"Oh, all over. North as well as South. We've got a whole basement vault full of index cards."

"I guess they're keeping close watch over it, aren't they?" asked Williams.

"Sure. It would take an army to get in that vault."

"Well, I guess they don't want anything to happen to the stuff before they spring it," observed the man from Republican headquarters.

Soon afterward Williams left Dr. Beard, took a stroll around the Anglo-Saxon Association's stately headquarters building, noted the half-dozen tough-looking guards about it and then caught the last train for the capital city. The next morning he had a long talk with Gorman Gay.

"It's okeh, Jo," he whispered to Bonds later, as he passed his desk.

ELEVEN

"What's the matter with you, Matt?" asked Bunny one morning about a month before election. "Ain't everything going okeh? You look as if we'd lost the election and failed to elect that brilliant intellectual, Henry Givens, President of the United States."

"Well, we might just as well lose it as far as I'm concerned," said Matthew, "if I don't find a way out of this jam I'm in."

"What jam?"

"Well, Helen got in the family way last winter again. I sent her to Palm Beach and the other resorts, thinking the travel and exercise might bring on another miscarriage."

"Did it?"

"Not a chance in the world. Then, to make matters worse, she miscalculates. At first she thought she would be confined in December; now she tells me she's only got about three weeks to go."

"Say not so!"

"I'm preaching gospel."

"Well, hush my mouth! Whaddya gonna do? You can't send her to one o' Crookman's hospitals, it would be too dangerous right now."

"That's just it. You see, I figured she wouldn't be ready until about a month after election when everything had calmed down, and I could send her then."

"Would she have gone?"

"She couldn't afford not to with her old man the President of the United States."

"Well, whaddya gonna do, Big Boy? Think fast! Think fast! Them three weeks will get away from here in no time."

"Don't I know it?"

"What about an abortion?" suggested Bunny, hopefully.

"Nothing doing. First place, she's too frail, and second place she's got some fool idea about that being a sin."

"About the only thing for you to do then," said Bunny, "is to get ready to pull out when that kid is born."

"Oh, Bunny, I'd hate to leave Helen. She's really the only woman I ever loved, you know. 'Course she's got her prejudices and queer notions like everybody else but she's really a little queen. She's been an inspiration to me, too, Bunny. Every time I talk about pulling out of this game when things don't go just right, she makes me stick it out. I guess I'd have been gone after I cleaned up that first million if it hadn't been for her."

"You'd have been better off if you had," Bunny commented.

"Oh, I don't know. She's hot for me to become Secretary of State or Ambassador to England or something like that; and the way things are going it looks like I will be. That is, if I can get out of this fix."

"If you can get out o' this jam, Matt, I'll sure take my hat off to you. An' I know how you feel about scuttling out and leaving her. I had a broad like that once in Harlem. 'Twas through her I got that job in th' bank. She was crazy about me, Boy, until she caught me two-timin'. Then she tried to shoot me."

"Squaws are funny that way," Bunny continued, philosophically. "Since I've been white I've found out they're all the same, white or black. Kipling was right. They'll fight to get you, fight to keep you and fight you when they catch you playin' around. But th' kinda woman that won't fight for a man ain't worth havin'."

"So you think I ought to pull out, eh Bunny?" asked the worried Matthew, returning to the subject.

"Well, what I'd suggest is this," his plump friend advised, "about time you think Helen's gonna be confined, get together as much cash as you can and keep your plane ready. Then, when the baby's born, go to her, tell her everything an' offer to take her away with you. If she won't go, you beat it; if she will, why everything's hotsy totsy." Bunny extended his soft pink hands expressively.

"Well, that sounds pretty good, Bunny."

"It's your best bet, Big Boy," said his friend and secretary.

Two days before election the situation was unchanged. There was joy in the Democratic camp, gloom among the Republicans. For the first time in American history it seemed that money was not going to decide an election. The propagandists and publicity men of the Democrats had so played upon the fears and prejudices of the public that even the bulk of Jews and Catholics were wavering and many had been won over to the support of a candidate who had denounced them but a few months before. In this they were but running true to form, however, as they had usually been on the side of white supremacy in the old days when there was a Negro population observable to the eye. The Republicans sought to dig up some scandal against Givens and Snobbcraft but were dissuaded by their Committee on Strategy which feared to set so dangerous a precedent. There were also politicians in their ranks who were guilty of adulteries, drunkenness and grafting.

The Republicans, Goosie and Gump, and the Democrats, Givens and Snobbcraft, had ended their swings around the country and were resting from their labors. There were parades in every city and country town. Minor orators beat the lectern from the Atlantic to the Pacific extolling the imaginary virtues of the candidates of the party that hired them. Dr. Crookman was burned a hundred times in effigy. Several lying-in hospitals were attacked. Two hundred citizens who knew nothing about either candidate were arrested for fighting over which was the better man.

The air was electric with expectancy. People stood around in knots. Small boys scattered leaflets on ten million doorsteps. Police were on the alert to suppress disorder, except what they created.

Arthur Snobbcraft, jovial and confident that he would soon assume a position befitting a member of one of the First Families of Virginia, was holding a brilliant pre-election party in his palatial residence. Strolling in and out amongst his guests, the master of the house accepted their premature congratulations in good humor. It was fine to hear oneself already addressed as Mr. Vice-President.

The tall English butler hastily edged his way through the throng surrounding the President of the Anglo-Saxon Association and whispered, "Dr. Buggerie is in the study upstairs. He says he must see you at once; that it is very, very important."

Puzzled, Snobbcraft went up to find out what in the world could be the trouble. As he entered, the massive statistician was striding back and forth, mopping his brow, his eyes starting from his head, a sheaf of typewritten sheets trembling in his hand.

"What's wrong, Buggerie?" asked Snobbcraft, perturbed.

"Everything! Everything!" shrilled the statistician.

"Be specific, please."

"Well," shaking the sheaf of papers in Snobbcraft's face, "we can't release any of this stuff! It's too damaging! It's too inclusive! We'll have to suppress it, Snobbcraft. You hear me? We mustn't let anyone get hold of it." The big man's flabby jowls worked excitedly.

"What do you mean?" snarled the F. F. V. "Do you mean to tell me that all of that money and work is wasted?"

"That's exactly what I mean," squeaked Buggerie. "It would be suicidal to publish it."

"Why? Get down to brass tacks, man, for God's sake. You get my goat."

"Now listen here, Snobbcraft," replied the statistician soberly, dropping heavily into a chair. "Sit down and listen to me. I started this investigation on the theory that the data gathered would prove that around twenty million people, mostly of the lower classes, were of Negro ancestry, recent and remote, while about half that number would be of uncertain or unknown ancestry."

"Well, what have you found?" insisted Snobbcraft, impatiently.

"I have found," continued Buggerie, "that over half the population has no record of its ancestry beyond five generations!"

"That's fine!" chortled Snobbcraft. "I've always maintained that there were only a few people of good blood in this country."

"But those figures include all classes," protested the larger man. "Your class as well as the lower classes."

"Don't insult me, Buggerie!" shouted the head of the Anglo-Saxons, half rising from his seat on the sofa.

"Be calm! Be calm!" cried Buggerie excitedly. "You haven't heard anything yet."

"What else, in the name of God, could be a worse libel on the aristocracy of this state?" Snobbcraft mopped his dark and haughty countenance.

"Well, these statistics we've gathered prove that most of our social leaders, especially of Anglo-Saxon lineage, are descendants of colonial stock that came here in bondage. They associated with slaves, in many cases worked and slept with them. They intermixed with the blacks and the women were sexually exploited by their masters. Then, even more than today, the illegitimate birth rate was very high in America."

Snobbcraft's face was working with suppressed rage. He started to rise but reconsidered. "Go on," he commanded.

"There was so much of this mixing between whites and blacks of the various classes that very early the colonies took steps to put a halt to it. They managed to prevent intermarriage but they couldn't stop intermixture. You know the old records don't lie. They're right there for everybody to see. . . .

"A certain percentage of these Negroes," continued Buggerie, quite at ease now and seemingly enjoying his dissertation, "in time lightened sufficiently to be able to pass for white. They then merged with the general population. Assuming that there were one thousand such cases fifteen generations ago—and we have proof that there were more—their descendants now number close to fifty million souls. Now I maintain that we dare not risk publishing this information. Too many of our very first families are touched right here in Richmond!"

"Buggerie!" gasped the F. F. V., "Are you mad?"

"Quite sane, sir," squeaked the ponderous man, somewhat proudly, "and I know what I know." He winked a watery eye.

"Well, go on. Is there any more?"

"Plenty," proceeded the statistician, amiably. "Take your own family, for instance. (Now don't get mad, Snobbcraft.) Take your own family. It is true that your people descended from King Alfred, but he has scores, perhaps hundreds of thousands, of descendants. Some are, of course, honored and respected citizens, cultured aristocrats who are a credit to the country; but most of them, my dear, dear Snobbcraft, are in what you call the lower orders: that is to say, laboring people, convicts, prostitutes, and that sort. One of your maternal ancestors in the late seventeenth century was the offspring of an English serving maid and a black slave. This woman in turn had a daughter by the plantation owner. This daughter was married to a former indentured slave. Their children were all white and you are one of their direct descendants!" Buggerie beamed.

"Stop!" shouted Snobbcraft, the veins standing out on his

narrow forehead and his voice trembling with rage. "You can't sit there and insult my family that way, suh."

"Now that outburst just goes to prove my earlier assertion," the large man continued, blandly. "If you get so excited about the truth, what do you think will be the reaction of other people? There's no use getting angry at me. I'm not responsible for your ancestry! Nor, for that matter, are you. You're no worse off than I am, Snobbcraft. My great, great grandfather had his ears cropped for non-payment of debts and was later jailed for thievery. His illegitimate daughter married a free Negro who fought in the Revolutionary War." Buggerie wagged his head almost gleefully.

"How can you admit it?" asked the scandalized Snobbcraft.

"Why not?" demanded Buggerie. "I have plenty of company. There's Givens, who is quite a fanatic on the race question and white supremacy, and yet he's only four generations removed from a mulatto ancestor."

"Givens too?"

"Yes, and also the proud Senator Kretin. He boasts, you know, of being descended from Pocahontas and Captain John Smith, but so are thousands of Negroes. Incidentally, there hasn't been an Indian unmixed with Negro on the Atlantic coastal plain for over a century and a half."

"What about Matthew Fisher?"

"We can find no record whatever of Fisher, which is true of about twenty million others, and so," he lowered his voice dramatically, "I have reason to suspect that he is one of those Negroes who have been whitened."

"And to think that I entertained him in my home!" Snobbcraft muttered to himself. And then aloud: "Well, what are we to do about it?"

"We must destroy the whole shooting match," the big man announced as emphatically as possible for one with a soprano voice, "and we'd better do it at once. The sooner we get through with it the better."

"But I can't leave my guests," protested Snobbcraft. Then

turning angrily upon his friend, he growled, "Why in the devil didn't you find all of this out before?"

"Well," said Buggerie, meekly, "I found out as soon as I could. We had to arrange and correlate the data, you know."

"How do you imagine we're going to get rid of that mountain of paper at this hour?" asked Snobbcraft, as they started down stairs.

"We'll get the guards to help us," said Buggerie, hopefully. "And we'll have the cards burned in the furnace."

"All right, then," snapped the F. F. V., "let's go and get it over with."

In five minutes they were speeding down the broad avenue to the headquarters of the Anglo-Saxon Association of America. They parked the car in front of the gate and walked up the cinder road to the front door. It was a balmy, moonlit night, almost as bright as day. They looked around but saw no one.

"I don't see any of the guards around," Snobbcraft remarked, craning his neck. "I wonder where they are?"

"Probably they're inside," Buggerie suggested, "although I remember telling them to patrol the outside of the building."

"Well, we'll go in, anyhow," remarked Snobbcraft. "Maybe they're down stairs."

He unlocked the door, swung it open and they entered. The hall was pitch dark. Both men felt along the wall for the button for the light. Suddenly there was a thud and Snobbcraft cursed.

"What's the matter?" wailed the frightened Buggerie, frantically feeling for a match.

"Turn on the God damned light!" roared Snobbcraft. "I just stumbled over a man. . . . Hurry up, will you?"

Dr. Buggerie finally found a match, struck it, located the wall button and pressed it. The hall was flooded with light. There arranged in a row on the floor and neatly trussed up and gagged were the six special guards.

"What the hell does this mean?" yelled Snobbcraft at the

mute men prone before them. Buggerie quickly removed the gags.

They had been suddenly set upon, the head watchman explained, about an hour before, just after Dr. Buggerie left, by a crowd of gunmen who had blackjacked them into unconsciousness and carried them into the building. The watchman displayed the lumps on their heads as evidence and looked quite aggrieved. Not one of them could remember what transpired after the sleep-producing buffet.

"The vault!" shrilled Buggerie. "Let's have a look at the vault."

Down the stairs they rushed, Buggerie wheezing in the lead, Snobbcraft following and the six tousled watchmen bringing up the rear. The lights in the basement were still burning brightly. The doors of the vault were open, sagging on their hinges. There was a litter of trash in front of the vault. They all clustered around the opening and peered inside. The vault was absolutely empty.

"My God!" exclaimed Snobbcraft and Buggerie in unison, turning two shades paler.

For a second or two they just gazed at each other. Then suddenly Buggerie smiled.

"That stuff won't do them any good," he remarked triumphantly.

"Why not?" demanded Snobbcraft, in his tone a mixture of eagerness, hope and doubt.

"Well, it will take them as long to get anything out of that mass of cards as it took our staff, and by that time you and Givens will be elected and no one will dare publish anything like that," the statistician explained. "I have in my possession the only summary—those papers I showed you at your house. As long as I've got that document and they haven't, we're all right!" he grinned in obese joy.

"That sounds good," sighed Snobbcraft, contentedly. "By the way, where is that summary?"

Buggerie jumped as if stuck by a pin and looked first into

his empty hands, then into his coat pockets and finally his trousers pockets. He turned and dashed out to the car, followed by the grim-looking Snobbcraft and the six uniformed watchmen with their tousled hair and sore bumps. They searched the car in vain, Snobbcraft loudly cursing Buggerie's stupidity.

"I—I must have left it in your study," wept Buggerie, meekly and hopefully. "In fact I think I remember leaving it right there on the table."

The enraged Snobbcraft ordered him into the car and they drove off leaving the six uniformed watchmen gaping at the entrance to the grounds, the moonbeams playing through their tousled hair.

The two men hit the ground almost as soon as the car crunched to a stop, dashed up the steps, into the house, through the crowd of bewildered guests, up the winding colonial stairs, down the hallway and into the study.

Buggerie switched on the light and looked wildly, hopefully around. Simultaneously the two men made a grab for a sheaf of white paper lying on the sofa. The statistician reached it first and gazed hungrily, gratefully at it. Then his eyes started from his head and his hand trembled.

"Look!" he shrieked dolefully, thrusting the sheaf of paper under Snobbcraft's eyes.

All of the sheets were blank except the one on top. On that was scribbled:

Thanks very much for leaving that report where I could get hold of it. Am leaving this paper so you'll have something on which to write another summary.

Happy dreams, Little One.

G.O.P.

"Great God!" gasped Snobbcraft, sinking into a chair.

TWELVE

The afternoon before election Matthew and Bunny sat in the latter's hotel suite sipping cocktails, smoking and awaiting the inevitable. They had been waiting ever since the day before. Matthew, tall and tense; Bunny, rotund and apprehensive, trying every so often to cheer up his chief with poor attempts at jocosity. Every time they heard a bell ring both jumped for the telephone, thinking it might be an announcement from Helen's bedside that an heir, and a dark one, had been born. When they could no longer stay around the office, they had come down to the hotel. In just a few moments they were planning to go back to the office again.

The hard campaign and the worry over the outcome of Helen's confinement had left traces on Matthew's face. The satanic lines were accentuated, the eyes seemed sunken farther back in the head, his well-manicured hand trembled a little as he reached for his glass again and again.

He wondered how it would all come out. He hated to leave. He had had such a good time since he'd been white: plenty of money, almost unlimited power, a beautiful wife, good liquor and the pick of damsels within reach. Must he leave all that? Must he cut and run just at the time when he was about to score his greatest victory. Just think: from an underpaid insurance agent to a millionaire commanding millions of people—and then oblivion. He shuddered slightly and reached again for his glass.

"I got everything fixed," Bunny remarked, shifting around

in the overstuffed chair. "The plane's all ready with tanks full and I've got Ruggles right there in the hangar. The money's in that little steel box: all in thousand dollar bills."

"You're going with me, aren't you, Bunny?" asked Matthew in almost pleading tones.

"I'm not stayin' here!" his secretary replied.

"Gee, Bunny, you're a brick!" said Matthew, leaning over and placing his hand on his plump little friend's knee. "You sure have been a good pal."

"Aw, cut th' comedy," exclaimed Bunny, reddening and turning his head swiftly away.

Suddenly the telephone rang, loud, clear, staccato. Both men sprang for it, eagerly, open-eyed, apprehensive. Matthew was first.

"Hello!" he shouted. "What's that! Yes, I'll be right up."

"Well, it's happened," he announced resignedly, hanging up the receiver. And then, brightening a bit, he boasted, "It's a boy!"

In the midst of her pain Helen was jubilant. What a present to give her Matthew on the eve of his greatest triumph! How good the Lord was to her; to doubly bless her in this way. The nurse wiped the tears of joy away from the young mother's eyes.

"You must stay quiet, Ma'am," she warned.

Outside in the hall, squirming uneasily on the window seat, was Matthew, his fists clenched, his teeth biting into his thin lower lip. At another window stood Bunny looking vacantly out into the street, feeling useless and out of place in such a situation, and yet convinced that it was his duty to stay here by his best friend during this great crisis.

Matthew felt like a young soldier about to leave his trench to face a baptism of machine gun fire or a gambler risking his last dollar on a roll of the dice. It seemed to him that he would go mad if something didn't happen quickly. He rose and paced the hall, hands in pockets, his tall shadow following him on the opposite wall. Why didn't the doctor come out and tell him something? What was the cause of the delay? What would Helen say? What would the baby look like? Maybe it might be miraculously light! Stranger things had happened in this world. But no, nothing like that could happen. Well, he'd had his lucky break; now the vacation was over.

A nurse, immaculate in white uniform, came out of Helen's bedroom, passed them hurriedly, smiling, and entered the bathroom. She returned with a basin of warm water in her hands, smiled again reassuringly and reëntered the natal chamber. Bunny and Matthew, in unison, sighed heavily.

"Boy!" exclaimed Bunny, wiping the perspiration from his brow. "If somethin' don't happen pretty soon here, I'm gonna do a Brodie out o' that window."

"The both of us," said Matthew. "I never knew it took these doctors so damn long to get through."

Helen's door opened and the physician came out looking quite grave and concerned. Matthew pounced upon him. The man held his finger to his lips and motioned to the room across the hall. Matthew entered.

"Well," said Matthew, guiltily, "what's the news?"

"I'm very sorry to have to tell you, Mr. Fisher, that something terrible has happened. Your son is very, very dark. Either you or Mrs. Fisher must possess some Negro blood. It might be called reversion to type if any such thing had ever been proved. Now I want to know what you want done. If you say so I can get rid of this child and it will save everybody concerned a lot of trouble and disgrace. Nobody except the nurse knows anything about this and she'll keep her mouth shut for a consideration. Of course, it's all in the day's work for me, you know. I've had plenty of cases like this in Atlanta, even before the disappearance of the Negroes. Come now, what shall I do?" he wailed.

"Yes," thought Matthew to himself, "what should he do?" The doctor had suggested an excellent way out of the dilemma. They could just say that the child had died. But what of the future? Must he go on forever in this way? Helen was young and fecund. Surely one couldn't go on murdering one's children, especially when one loved and wanted children. Wouldn't it be better to settle the matter once and for all? Or should he let the doctor murder the boy and then hope for a better situation the next time? An angel of frankness beckoned him to be done with this life of pretense; to take his wife and son and flee far away from everything, but a devil of ambition whispered seductively about wealth, power and prestige.

In almost as many seconds the pageant of the past three years passed in review on the screen of his tortured memory: the New Year's Eve at the Honky Tonk Club, the first glimpse of the marvelously beautiful Helen, the ordeal of getting white, the first, sweet days of freedom from the petty insults and cheap discriminations to which as a black man he had always been subjected, then the search for Helen around Atlanta, the organization of the Knights of Nordica, the stream of successes, the coming of Bunny, the campaign planned and executed by him: and now, the end. Must it be the end?

"Well?" came the insistent voice of the physician.

Matthew opened his mouth to reply when the butler burst into the room waving a newspaper.

"Excuse me, sir," he blurted, excitedly, "but Mister Brown said to bring this right to you."

The lurid headlines seemed to leap from the paper and strike Matthew between the eyes:

DEMOCRATIC LEADERS
PROVED OF NEGRO DESCENT
GIVENS, SNOBBCRAFT, BUGGERIE, KRETIN AND OTHERS OF NEGRO ANCESTRY, ACCORDING TO OLD RECORDS UNEARTHED BY THEM.

Matthew and the physician, standing side by side, read the long account in awed silence. Bunny entered the door.

"Can I speak to you a minute, Matt?" he asked casually. Almost reluctant to move, Matthew followed him into the hall.

"Keep your shirt on, Big Boy," Bunny advised, almost jovially. "They ain't got nothin' on you yet. That changing your name threw them off. You're not even mentioned."

Matthew braced up, threw back his shoulders and drew a long, deep breath. It seemed as if a mountain had been taken off his shoulders. He actually grinned as his confidence returned. He reached for Bunny's hand and they shook, silently jubilant.

"Well, Doctor," said Matthew, arching his left eyebrow in his familiar Mephistophelian manner, "it sort of looks as if there is something to that reversion to type business. I used to think it was all baloney myself. Well, it's as I always say: you never can tell."

"Yes, it seems as if this is a very authentic case," agreed the physician, glancing sharply at the bland and blond countenance of Matthew. "Well, what now?"

"I'll have to see Givens," said Matthew as they turned to leave the room.

"Here he comes now," Bunny announced.

Sure enough, the little gray-faced, bald-headed man came leaping up the stairs like a goat, his face haggard, his eyes bulging in mingled rage and terror, his necktie askew. He was waving a newspaper in his hand and opened his mouth without speaking as he shot past them and dashed into Helen's room. The old fellow was evidently out of his head.

They followed him into a room in time to see him with his face buried in the covers of Helen's bed and she, horrified, glancing at the six-inch-tall headline. Matthew rushed to her side as she slumped back on the pillow in a dead faint. The physician and nurse dashed to revive her. The old man on his knees sobbed hoarsely. Mrs. Givens looking fifteen years older appeared in the doorway. Bunny glanced at Matthew who slightly lowered his left eyelid and with difficulty suppressed a smile.

"We've got to get out o' this!" shouted the Imperial Grand Wizard. "We've got to get out o' this, Oh, it's terrible. . . . I never knew it myself, for sure. . . . Oh, Matthew, get us out of this, I tell you. They almost mobbed me at the office. . . . Came in just as I went out the back way. . . . Almost ten thousand of them. . . . We can't lose a minute. Quick, I tell you! They'll murder us all."

"I'll look out for everything," Matthew soothed condescendingly. "I'll stick by you." Then turning swiftly to his partner he commanded, "Bunny order both cars out at once. We'll beat it for the airport. . . . Doctor Brocker, will you go with us to look out for Helen and the baby? We've got to get out right now. I'll pay you your price."

"Sure I'll go, Mr. Fisher," said the physician, quietly. "I wouldn't leave Mrs. Fisher now."

The nurse had succeeded in bringing Helen to consciousness. She was weeping bitterly, denouncing fate and her father. With that logicality that frequently causes people to accept as truth circumstantial evidence that is not necessarily conclusive, she was assuming that the suspiciously brown color of her new-born son was due to some hidden Negro drop of blood in her veins. She looked up at her husband beseechingly.

"Oh, Matthew, darling," she cried, her long red-gold hair framing her face, "I'm so sorry about all this. If I'd only known, I'd never have let you in for it. I would have spared you this disgrace and humiliation. Oh, Matthew, Honey, please forgive me. I love you, my husband. Please don't leave me, please don't leave me. I love you, my husband. Please don't leave me, please don't leave me!" She reached out and grasped the tail of his coat as if he were going to leave that very minute.

"Now, now, little girl," said Matthew soothingly, touched by her words. "You haven't disgraced me; you've honored me by presenting me with a beautiful son."

He looked down worshipfully at the chubby ball of brownness in the nurse's arms.

"You needn't worry about me, Helen. I'll stick by you as long as you'll have me and without you life wouldn't be worth a dime. You're not responsible for the color of our baby, my dear. I'm the guilty one."

Dr. Brocker smiled knowingly, Givens rose up indignantly, Bunny opened his mouth in surprise, Mrs. Givens folded her arms and her mouth changed to a slit and the nurse said, "Oh!"

"You?" cried Helen in astonishment.

"Yes, me," Matthew repeated, a great load lifting from his soul. Then for a few minutes he poured out his secret to the astonished little audience.

Helen felt a wave of relief go over her. There was no feeling of revulsion at the thought that her husband was a Negro. There once would have been but that was seemingly centuries ago when she had been unaware of her remoter Negro ancestry. She felt proud of her Matthew. She loved him more than ever. They had money and a beautiful, brown baby. What more did they need? To hell with the world! To hell with society! Compared to what she possessed, thought Helen, all talk of race and color was damned foolishness. She would probably have been surprised to learn that countless Americans at that moment were thinking the same thing.

"Well," said Bunny, grinning, "it sure is good to be able to admit that you're a jigwalk once more."

"Yes, Bunny," said old man Givens, "I guess we're all niggers now."

"Negroes, Mr. Givens, Negroes," corrected Dr. Brocker, entering the room. "I'm in the same boat with the rest of you, only my dark ancestors are not so far back. I sure hope the Republicans win."

"Don't worry, Doc," said Bunny. "They'll win all right. And how! Gee whiz! I bet Sherlock Holmes, Nick Carter and all the Pinkertons couldn't find old Senator Kretin and Arthur Snobbcraft now."

"Come on," shouted the apprehensive Givens, "let's get out o' here before that mob comes."

"Whut mob, Daddy?" asked Mrs. Givens.

"You'll find out damn quick if you don't shake it up," replied her husband.

Through the crisp, autumn night air sped Fisher's big tri-motored plane, headed southwest to the safety of Mexico. Reclining in a large, comfortable deck chair was Helen Fisher, calm and at peace with the world. In a hammock near her was her little brown son, Matthew, Junior. Beside her, holding her hand, was Matthew. Up front near the pilot, Bunny and Givens were playing Conquian. Behind them sat the nurse and Dr. Brocker, silently gazing out of the window at the twinkling lights of the Gulf Coast. Old lady Givens snored in the rear of the ship.

"Damn!" muttered Givens, as Bunny threw down his last spread and won the third consecutive game. "I sure wish I'd had time to grab some jack before we pulled out o' Atlanta. Ain't got but five dollars and fifty-three cents to my name."

"Don't worry about that, Old Timer," Bunny laughed. "I don't think we left over a thousand bucks in the treasury. See that steel box over there? Well, that ain't got nothin' in it but bucks and more bucks. Not a bill smaller than a grand."

"Well, I'm a son-of-a-gun," blurted the Imperial Grand Wizard. "That boy thinks o' everything."

But Givens was greatly depressed, much more so than the others. He had really believed all that he had preached about white supremacy, race purity and the menace of the alien, the Catholic, the Modernist and the Jew. He had always been sincere in his prejudices.

When they arrived at the Valbuena Air Field outside Mexico City, a messenger brought Bunny a telegram.

"You better thank your stars you got away from there, Matt," he grinned, handing his friend the telegram. "See what my gal says?"

Matthew glanced over the message and handed it to Givens without comment. It read:

Hope you arrive safely Stop Senator Kretin lynched in Union Station Stop Snobbcraft and Buggerie reported in flight Stop Goosie and Gump almost unanimously reëlected Stop Government has declared martial law until disturbances stop Stop When can I come?

MADELINE SCRANTON.

"Who's this Scranton broad?" queried Matthew in a whisper, cutting a precautionary glance at his wife.

"A sweet Georgia brown," exclaimed Bunny enthusiastically.

"No!" gasped Matthew, incredulous.

"She ain't no Caucasian!" Bunny replied.

"She must be the last black gal in the country," Matthew remarked, glancing enviously at his friend. "How come she didn't get white, too?"

"Well," Bunny replied, a slight hint of pride in his voice. "She's a race patriot. She's funny that way."

"Well, for cryin' out loud!" exclaimed Matthew, scratching his head and sort of half grinning in a bewildered way. "*What* kind o' *sheba* is that?"

Old man Givens came over to where they were standing, the telegram in his hand and an expression of serenity now on his face.

"Boys," he announced, "it looks like it's healthier down here right now than it is back there in Georgia."

"*Looks* like it's healthier?" mocked Bunny. "Brother, you know damn *well* it's healthier!"

THIRTEEN

Toward eleven o'clock on the evening before election day, a long, low roadster swept up to the door of a stately country home near Richmond, Va., crunched to a stop, the lights were extinguished and two men, one tall and angular, the other huge and stout, catapulted from the car. Without wasting words, they raced around the house and down a small driveway to a rambling shed in a level field about three hundred yards to the rear. Breathless, they halted before the door and beat upon it excitedly.

"Open up there, Frazier!" ordered Snobbcraft, for it was he. "Open that door." There was no answer. The only reply was the chirping of crickets and the rustle of branches.

"He must not be here," said Dr. Buggerie, glancing fearfully over his shoulder and wiping a perspiring brow with a damp handkerchief.

"The damned rascal had better be here," thundered the Democratic candidate for Vice-President, beating again on the door. "I telephoned him two hours ago to be ready."

As he spoke someone unlocked the door and rolled it aside an inch or two.

"Is that you, Mr. Snobbcraft?" asked a sleepy voice from the darkness within.

"Open that damned door, you fool," barked Snobbcraft. "Didn't I tell you to have that plane ready when we got here? Why don't you do as you're told?" He and Dr. Buggerie helped slide the great doors back. The man Frazier snapped on the lights, revealing within a big, three-motored plane with an automobile nestling under each of its wings.

"I-I kinda fell asleep waitin' for you, Mr. Snobbcraft," Frazier apologized, "but everything's ready."

"All right, man," shouted the president of the Anglo-Saxon Association, "let's get away from here then. This is a matter of life and death. You ought to have had the plane outside and all warmed up to go."

"Yes sir," the man mumbled meekly, busying himself.

"These damned, stupid, poor white trash!" growled Snobbcraft, glaring balefully at the departing aviator.

"D-D-Don't antagonize him," muttered Buggerie. "He's our only chance to get away."

"Shut up, fool! If it hadn't been for you and your damned fool statistics we wouldn't be in this fix."

"You wanted them, didn't you?" whined the statistician in defense.

"Well, I didn't tell you to leave that damned summary where anybody could get hold of it." Snobbcraft replied, reproachfully. "That was the most stupid thing I ever heard of."

Buggerie opened his mouth to reply but said nothing. He just glared at Snobbcraft who glared back at him. The two men presented a disheveled appearance. The Vice-Presidential candidate was haggard, hatless, collarless and still wore his smoking jacket. The eminent statistician and author of *The Incidence of Psittacosis among the Hiphopa Indians of the Amazon Valley and Its Relation to Life Insurance Rates in the United States* looked far from dignified with no necktie, canvas breeches, no socks and wearing a shooting jacket he had snatched from a closet on his way out of the house. He had forgotten his thick spectacles and his bulging eyes were red and watery. They paced impatiently back and forth, glancing first at the swiftly working Frazier and then down the long driveway toward the glowing city.

Ten minutes they waited while Frazier went over the plane to see that all was well. Then they helped him roll the huge metal bird out of the hangar and onto the field. Gratefully they climbed inside and fell exhausted on the soft-cushioned seats.

"Well, that sure is a relief," gasped the ponderous Buggerie, mopping his brow.

"Wait until we get in the air," growled Snobbcraft. "Anything's liable to happen after that mob tonight. I was never so humiliated in my life. The idea of that gang of poor white trash crowding up my steps and yelling nigger. It was disgraceful."

"Yes, it was terrible," agreed Buggerie. "It's a good thing they didn't go in the rear where your car was. We wouldn't have been able to get away."

"I thought there would be a demonstration," said Snobbcraft, some of his old sureness returning, "that's why I 'phoned Frazier to get ready. . . . Oh, it's a damned shame to be run out of your own home in this way!"

He glared balefully at the statistician who averted his gaze.

"All ready, sir," announced Frazier, "where are we headed?"

"To my ranch in Chihuahua, and hurry up," snapped Snobbcraft.

"But—But we ain't got enough gas to go that far," said Frazier. "I-I-You didn't say you wanted to go to Mexico, Boss."

Snobbcraft stared incredulously at the man. His rage was so great that he could not speak for a moment or two. Then he launched into a stream of curses that would have delighted a pirate captain, while the unfortunate aviator gaped indecisively.

In the midst of this diatribe, the sound of automobile horns and klaxons rent the air, punctuated by shouts and pistol shots. The three men in the plane saw coming down the road from the city a bobbing stream of headlights. Already the cavalcade was almost to the gate of the Snobbcraft country estate.

"Come on, get out of here," gasped Snobbcraft. "We'll get some gas farther down the line. Hurry up!"

Dr. Buggerie, speechless and purple with fear, pushed the aviator out of the plane. The fellow gave the propeller a whirl, jumped back into the cabin, took the controls and the great machine rolled out across the field.

They had started none too soon. The automobile cavalcade was already coming up the driveway. The drone of the motor drowned out the sound of the approaching mob but the two fearful men saw several flashes that betokened pistol shots. Several of the automobiles took out across the field in the wake of the plane. They seemed to gain on it. Snobbcraft and Buggerie gazed nervously ahead. They were almost at the end of the field and the plane had not yet taken to the air. The pursuing automobiles drew closer. There were several more flashes from firearms. A bullet tore through the side of the cabin. Simultaneously Snobbcraft and Buggerie fell to the floor.

At last the ship rose, cleared the trees at the end of the field and began to attain altitude. The two men took deep breaths of relief, rose and flung themselves on the richly upholstered seats.

A terrible stench suddenly became noticeable to the two passengers and the aviator. The latter looked inquiringly over his shoulder; Snobbcraft and Buggerie, their noses wrinkled and their foreheads corrugated, glanced suspiciously at each other. Both moved uneasily in their seats and looks of guilt succeeded those of accusation. Snobbcraft retreated precipitously to the rear cabin while the statistician flung open several windows and then followed the Vice-Presidential candidate.

Fifteen minutes later two bundles were tossed out of the window of the rear cabin and the two passengers, looking sheepish but much relieved, resumed their seats. Snobbcraft was wearing a suit of brown dungarees belonging to Frazier while his scientific friend had wedged himself into a pair of white trousers usually worn by Snobbcraft's valet. Frazier turned, saw them, and grinned.

Hour after hour the plane winged its way through the night. Going a hundred miles an hour it passed town after town. About dawn, as they were passing over Meridian, Mississippi, the motor began to miss.

"What's the matter there?" Snobbcraft inquired nervously into the pilot's ear.

"The gas is runnin' low," Frazier replied grimly. "We'll have to land pretty soon."

"No, no, not in Mississippi!" gasped Buggerie, growing purple with apprehension. "They'll lynch us if they find out who we are."

"Well, we can't stay up here much longer," the pilot warned.

Snobbcraft bit his lip and thought furiously. It was true they would be taking a chance by landing anywhere in the South, let alone in Mississippi, but what could they do? The motor was missing more frequently and Frazier had cut down their speed to save gasoline. They were just idling along. The pilot looked back at Snobbcraft inquiringly.

"By God, we're in a fix now," said the president of the Anglo-Saxon Association. Then he brightened with a sudden idea. "We could hide in the rear cabin while Frazier gets gasoline," he suggested.

"Suppose somebody looks in the rear cabin?" queried Buggerie, dolefully, thrusting his hands into the pockets of his white trousers. "There's bound to be a lot of curious people about when a big plane like this lands in a farming district."

As he spoke his left hand encountered something hard in the pocket. It felt like a box of salve. He withdrew it curiously. It was a box of shoe polish which the valet doubtless used on Snobbcraft's footgear. He looked at it aimlessly and was about to thrust it back into the pocket when he had a brilliant idea.

"Look here, Snobbcraft," he cried excitedly, his rheumy

eyes popping out of his head farther than usual. "This is just the thing."

"What do you mean?" asked his friend, eyeing the little tin box.

"Well," explained the scientist, "you know real niggers are scarce now and nobody would think of bothering a couple of them, even in Mississippi. They'd probably be a curiosity."

"What are you getting at, man?"

"This: we can put this blacking on our head, face, neck and hands, and no one will take us for Snobbcraft and Buggerie. Frazier can tell anybody that inquires that we're two darkies he's taking out of the country, or something like that. Then, after we get our gas and start off again, we can wash the stuff off with gasoline. It's our only chance, Arthur. If we go down like we are, they'll kill us sure."

Snobbcraft pursed his lips and pondered the proposition for a moment. It was indeed, he saw, their only chance to effectively escape detection.

"All right," he agreed, "let's hurry up. This ship won't stay up much longer."

Industriously they daubed each other's head, neck, face, chest, hands and arms with the shoe polish. In five minutes they closely resembled a brace of mammy singers. Snobbcraft hurriedly instructed Frazier.

The plane slowly circled to the ground. The region was slightly rolling and there was no good landing place. There could be no delay, however, so Frazier did his best. The big ship bumped over logs and through weeds, heading straight for a clump of trees. Quickly the pilot steered it to the left only to send it head first into a ditch. The plane turned completely over, one wing was entirely smashed and Frazier, caught in the wreckage under the engine, cried feebly for help for a few moments and then lay still.

Shaken up and bruised, the two passengers managed to crawl out of the cabin window to safety. Dolefully they stood in the Mississippi sunlight, surveying the wreckage and looking questioningly at each other.

"Well," whined Dr. Buggerie, rubbing one large sore buttock, "what now?"

"Shut up," growled Snobbcraft. "If it hadn't been for you, we wouldn't be here."

Happy Hill, Mississippi, was all aflutter. For some days it had been preparing for the great, open-air revival of the True Faith Christ Lovers' Church. The faithful for miles around were expected to attend the services scheduled for the afternoon of Election Day and which all hoped would last well into the night.

This section of the state had been untouched by the troubles through which the rest of the South had gone as a result of the activities of Black-No-More, Incorporated. The people for miles around were with very few exceptions old residents and thence known to be genuine blue-blooded Caucasians for as far back as any resident could remember which was at least fifty years. The people were proud of this fact. They were more proud, however, of the fact that Happy Hill was the home and birthplace of the True Faith Christ Lovers' Church, which made the prodigious boast of being the most truly Fundamentalist of all the Christian sects in the United States. Other things of which the community might have boasted were its inordinately high illiteracy rate and its lynching record—but these things were seldom mentioned, although no one was ashamed of them. Certain things are taken for granted everywhere.

Long before the United States had rid themselves of their Negroes through the good but unsolicited offices of Dr. Junius Crookman, Happy Hill had not only rid itself of what few Negroes had resided in its vicinity but of all itinerant blackamoors who lucklessly came through the place. Ever since the Civil War, when the proud and courageous forefathers of the Caucasian inhabitants had vigorously resisted all efforts to draft them into the Confederate Army, there had been a sign nailed over the general store and post office reading NIGER REDE & RUN. IF U CAN'T REDE, RUN ENEY-HOWE. The literate denizens of Happy Hill would sometimes stand off and spell out the words with the pride that usually accompanies erudition.

The method by which Happy Hill discouraged blacka-moors who sought the hospitality of the place was simple: the offending Ethiopian was either hung or shot and then broiled. Across from the general store and post office was a large iron post about five feet high. On it all blacks were burned. Down one side of it was a long line of nicks made with hammer and chisel. Each nick stood for a Negro dis-patched. This post was one of the landmarks of the commu-nity and was pointed out to visitors with pardonable civic pride by local boosters. Sage old fellows frequently remarked between expectorations of tobacco juice that the only Negro problem in Happy Hill was the difficulty of getting hold of a sufficient number of the Sons or Daughters of Ham to lighten the dullness of the place.

Quite naturally the news that all Negroes had disappeared, not only from their state but from the entire country, had been received with sincere regret by the inhabitants of Happy Hill. They envisioned the passing of an old, established custom. Now there was nothing left to stimulate them but the old time religion and the clandestine sex orgies that invariably and immediately followed the great revival meetings.

So the simple country folk had turned to religion with renewed ardor. There were several churches in the country, Methodist, Baptist, Campbellite and, of course, Holy Roller. The latter, indeed, had the largest membership. But the people, eager for something new, found all of the old churches too tame. They wanted a faith with more punch to it; a faith that would fittingly accompany the fierce corn liquor which all consumed, albeit they were all confirmed Prohibitionists.

Whenever and wherever there is a social need, some agency

arises to supply it. The needs of Happy Hill were no exception. One day, several weeks previously, there had come to the community one Rev. Alex McPhule who claimed to be the founder of a new faith, a true faith, that would save all from the machinations of the Evil One. The other churches, he averred, had failed. The other churches had grown soft and were flirting with atheism and Modernism which, according to Rev. McPhule, were the same thing. An angel of God had visited him one summer evening in Meridian, he told them, when he was down sick in bed as the result of his sinning ways, and had told him to reform and go forth into the world and preach the true faith of Christ's love. He had promised to do so, of course, and then the angel had placed the palm of his right hand on Rev. McPhule's forehead and all of the sickness and misery had departed.

The residents of Happy Hill and vicinity listened with rapt attention and respect. The man was sincere, eloquent and obviously a Nordic. He was tall, thin, slightly knock-kneed, with a shock of unkempt red hair, wild blue eyes, hollow cheeks, lantern jaw and long apelike arms that looked very impressive when he waved them up and down during a harangue. His story sounded logical to the country people and they flocked in droves to his first revival held in a picturesque natural amphitheater about a mile from town.

No one had any difficulty in understanding the new faith. No music was allowed besides singing and thumping the bottom of a wooden tub. There were no chairs. Everybody sat on the ground in a circle with Rev. McPhule in the center. The holy man would begin an extemporaneous song and would soon have the faithful singing it after him and swinging from side to side in unison. Then he would break off abruptly and launch into an old-fashion hellfire-and-damnation sermon in which demons, brimstone, adultery, rum, and other evils prominently figured. At the height of his remarks, he would roll his eyes heavenward, froth at the mouth, run around on all fours and embrace in turn

each member of the congregation, especially the buxom ladies. This would be the signal for others to follow his ex-
ample. The sisters and brothers osculated, embraced and
rolled, shouting meanwhile: "Christ is Love! . . . Love
Christ! . . . Oh, be happy in the arms of Jesus! . . . Oh, Jesus
my Sweetheart! . . . Heavenly Father!" Frequently these revivals took place on the darkest nights with the place of
worship dimly illuminated by pine torches. As these torches
always seemed to conveniently burn out about the time the
embracing and rolling started, the new faith rapidly became
popular.

In a very short time nothing in Happy Hill was too good
for Rev. Alex McPhule. Every latchstring hung out for him.
As usual with gentlemen of the cloth, he was especially popular with the ladies. When the men were at work in the fields,
the Man of God would visit house after house and comfort
the womenfolk with his Christian message. Being a bachelor,
he made these professional calls with great frequency.

The Rev. Alex McPhule also held private audiences with
the sick, sinful and neurotic in his little cabin. There he had
erected an altar covered with the white marble top from an
old bureau. Around this altar were painted some grotesque
figures, evidently the handiwork of the evangelist, while on
the wall in back of the altar hung a large square of white
oilcloth upon which was painted a huge eye. The sinner seeking surcease was commanded to gaze upon the eye while
making confessions and requests. On the altar reposed a
crudely-bound manuscript about three inches thick. This was
the "Bible" of the Christ Lovers which the Rev. McPhule
declared he had written at the command of Jesus Christ
Himself. The majority of his visitors were middle-aged wives
and adenoidal and neurotic young girls. None departed un-
satisfied.

With all the good fortune that had come to the Rev. McPhule as a result of engaging in the Lord's work, he was still
dissatisfied. He never passed a Baptist, Methodist or Holy

Roller church without jealousy and ambition surging up within him. He wanted everybody in the county in his flock. He wanted to do God's work so effectually that the other churches would be put out of business. He could only do this, he knew, with the aid of a message straight from Heaven. That alone would impress them.

He began to talk in his meetings about a sign coming down from Heaven to convince all doubters and infidels like Methodists and Baptists. His flock was soon on the nervous edge of expectancy but the Lord failed, for some reason, to answer the prayer of his right-hand man.

Rev. McPhule began to wonder what he had done to offend the Almighty. He prayed long and fervently in the quiet of his bedchamber, except when he didn't have company, but no sign appeared. Possibly, thought the evangelist, some big demonstration might attract the attention of Jesus; something bigger than the revivals he had been staging. Then one day somebody brought him a copy of *The Warning* and upon reading it he got an idea. If the Lord would only send him a nigger for his congregation to lynch! That would, indeed, be marked evidence of the power of Rev. Alex McPhule.

He prayed with increased fervency but no African put in an appearance. Two nights later as he sat before his altar, his "Bible" clutched in his hands, a bat flew in the window. It rapidly circled the room and flew out again. Rev. McPhule could feel the wind from its wings. He stood erect with a wild look in his watery blue eyes and screamed, "A sign! A sign! Oh, Glory be! The Lord has answered my prayer! Oh, thank you, God! A sign! A sign!" Then he grew dizzy, his eyes dimmed and he fell twitching across the altar, unconscious.

Next day he went around Happy Hill telling of his experience of the night before. An angel of the Lord, he told the gaping villagers, had flown through the window, alighted on his "Bible" and, kissing him on his forehead, had declared that the Lord would answer his prayer and send a sign. As proof of his tale, Rev. McPhule exhibited a red spot on his forehead which he had received when his head struck the marble altar top but which he claimed marked the place where the messenger of the Lord had kissed him.

The simple folk of Happy Hill were, with few exceptions, convinced that the Rev. McPhule stood in well with the celestial authorities. Nervous and expectant they talked of nothing but The Sign. They were on edge for the great revival scheduled for Election Day at which time they fervently hoped the Lord would make good.

At last the great day had arrived. From far and near came the good people of the countryside on horseback, in farm wagons and battered mudcaked flivvers. Many paused to cast their ballots for Givens and Snobbcraft, not having heard of the developments of the past twenty-four hours, but the bulk of the folk repaired immediately to the sacred groove where the preaching would take place.

Rev. Alex McPhule gloated inwardly at the many concentric circles of upturned faces. They were eager, he saw, to drink in his words of wisdom and be elevated. He noted with satisfaction that there were many strange people in the congregation. It showed that his power was growing. He glanced up apprehensively at the blue heavens. Would The Sign come? Would the Lord answer his prayers? He muttered another prayer and then proceeded to business.

He was an impressive figure today. He had draped himself in a long, white robe with a great red cross on the left breast and he looked not unlike one of the Prophets of old. He walked back and forth in the little circle surrounded by close-packed humanity, bending backward and forward, swinging his arms, shaking his head and rolling his eyes while he retold for the fiftieth time the story of the angel's visit. The man was a natural actor and his voice had that sepulchral tone universally associated with Men of God, court criers and Independence Day orators. In the first row squatted the Happy Hill True Faith Choir of eight young women and grizzled old man Yawbrew, the tub-thumper, among them. They groaned, amended, and Yes-Lorded at irregular intervals.

Then, having concluded his story, the evangelist launched into song in a harsh, nasal voice:

> I done come to Happy Hill to save you from sin,
> Salvation's door is open and you'd better come in,
> Oh, Glory Hallelujah! you'd better come in.
> Jesus Christ has called me to save this white race,
> And with His Help I'll save you from awful disgrace.
> Oh, Glory Hallelujah! We must save this race.

Old man Yawbrew beat on his tub while the sisters swayed and accompanied their pastor. The congregation joined in.

Suddenly Rev. McPhule stopped, glared at the rows of strained, upturned faces and extending his long arms to the sun, he shouted:

"It'll come I tell yuh. Yes Lord, the sign will come—ugh. I know that my Lord liveth and the sign will come—ugh. If—ugh—you just have faith—ugh. Oh, Jesus—ugh. Brothers and Sisters—ugh. Just have faith—ugh—and the Lord—ugh—will answer your prayers. . . . Oh, Christ—ugh. Oh, Little Jesus—ugh. . . . Oh, God—ugh—answer our prayers. . . . Save us—ugh. Send us the Sign. . . ."

The congregation shouted after him "Send us the Sign!" Then he again launched into a hymn composed on the spot:

> He will send the Sign,
> Oh, He will send the Sign
> Loving Little Jesus Christ
> He will send the Sign.

Over and over he sang the verse. The people joined him until the volume of sound was tremendous. Then with a piercing scream, Rev. McPhule fell on all fours and running among the people hugged one after the other, crying "Christ is Love! . . . He'll send the Sign! . . . Oh, Jesus! Send us The Sign!" The cries of the others mingled with his and there was a general kissing, embracing and rolling there in the green-walled grove under the midday sun.

As the sun approached its zenith, Mr. Arthur Snobbcraft and Dr. Samuel Buggerie, grotesque in their nondescript clothing and their blackened skins, trudged along the dusty road in what they hoped was the direction of a town. For three hours, now, they had been on the way, skirting isolated farmhouses and cabins, hoping to get to a place where they could catch a train. They had fiddled aimlessly around the wrecked plane for two or three hours before getting up courage enough to take to the highroad. Suddenly they both thrilled with pleasure somewhat dampened by apprehension as they espied from a rise in the road a considerable collection of houses.

"There's a town," exclaimed Snobbcraft. "Now let's get this damned stuff off our faces. There's probably a telegraph office there."

"Oh, don't be crazy," Buggerie pleaded. "If we take off this blacking we're lost. The whole country has heard the news about us by this time, even in Mississippi. Let's go right in as we are, pretending we're niggers, and I'll bet we'll be treated all right. We won't have to stay long. With our pictures all over the country, it would be suicidal to turn up here in one of these hotbeds of bigotry and ignorance."

"Well, maybe you're right," Snobbcraft grudgingly admitted. He was eager to get the shoe polish off his skin. Both men had perspired freely during their hike and the sweat had mixed with the blacking much to their discomfort.

As they started toward the little settlement, they heard shouts and singing on their left.

"What's that?" cried Dr. Buggerie, stopping to listen.

"Sounds like a camp meeting," Snobbcraft replied. "Hope

it is. We can be sure those folks will treat us right. One thing about these people down here they are real, sincere Christians."

"I don't think it will be wise to go where there's any crowds," warned the statistician. "You never can tell what a crowd will do."

"Oh, shut up, and come on!" Snobbcraft snapped. "I've listened to you long enough. If it hadn't been for you we would never have had all of this trouble. Statistics! Bah!"

They struck off over the fields toward the sound of the singing. Soon they reached the edge of the ravine and looked down on the assemblage. At about the same time, some of the people facing in that direction saw them and started yelling "The Sign! Look! Niggers! Praise God! The Sign! Lynch 'em!" Others joined in the cry. Rev. McPhule turned loose a buxom sister and stood wide-eyed and erect. His prayers had come true! "Lynch 'em!" he roared.

"We'd better get out of here," said Buggerie, quaking.

"Yes," agreed Snobbcraft, as the assemblage started to move toward them.

Over fences, through bushes, across ditches sped the two men, puffing and wheezing at the unaccustomed exertion, while in hot pursuit came Rev. McPhule followed by his enthusiastic flock.

Slowly the mob gained on the two Virginia aristocrats. Dr. Buggerie stumbled and sprawled on the ground. A dozen men and women fell upon him while he yelled to the speeding Snobbcraft for help. The angular Snobbcraft kept on but Rev. McPhule and several others soon overtook him.

The two men were marched protesting to Happy Hill. The enthused villagers pinched them, pulled them, playfully punched and kicked them during their triumphant march. No one paid the slightest attention to their pleas. Too long had Happy Hill waited for a Negro to lynch. Could the good people hesitate now that the Lord had answered their prayers?

Buggerie wept and Snobbcraft offered large sums of money

for their freedom. The money was taken and distributed but the two men were not liberated. They insisted that they were not Negroes but they were only cudgeled for their pains.

At last the gay procession arrived at the long-unused iron post in front of the general store and post office in Happy Hill. As soon as Mr. Snobbcraft saw the post he guessed its significance. Something must be done quickly.

"We're not niggers," he yelled to the mob. "Take off our clothes and look at us. See for yourself. My God! Don't lynch white men. We're white the same as you are."

"Yes, gentlemen," bleated Dr. Buggerie, "we're really white men. We just came from a masquerade ball over at Meridian and our plane wrecked. You can't do a thing like this. We're white men, I tell you."

The crowd paused. Even Rev. McPhule seemed convinced. Eager hands tore off the men's garments and revealed their pale white skins underneath. Immediately apology took the place of hatred. The two men were taken over to the general store and permitted to wash off the shoe polish while the crowd, a little disappointed, stood around wondering what to do. They felt cheated. Somebody must be to blame for depriving them of their fun. They began to eye Rev. McPhule. He glanced around nervously.

Suddenly, in the midst of this growing tenseness, an ancient Ford drove up to the outskirts of the crowd and a young man jumped out waving a newspaper.

"Looky here!" he yelled. "They've found out th' damned Demmycratic candidates is niggers. See here: Givens and Snobbcraft. Them's their pictures. They pulled out in airplanes last night or th' mobs wouldda lynched 'em." Men, women and children crowded around the newcomer while he read the account of the flight of the Democratic standard bearers. They gazed at each other bewildered and hurled imprecations upon the heads of the vanished candidates.

Washed and refreshed, Mr. Arthur Snobbcraft and Dr. Samuel Buggerie, each puffing a five-cent cigar (the most expensive sold in the store) appeared again on the porch of the general store. They felt greatly relieved after their narrow escape.

"I told you they wouldn't know who we were," said Snobbcraft disdainfully but softly.

"Who are you folks, anyway?" asked Rev. McPhule, suddenly at their elbow. He was holding the newspaper in his hand. The crowd was watching breathlessly.

"Why-why-y I'm-a-er-a that is . . ." spluttered Snobbcraft.

"Ain't that your pichure?" thundered the evangelist, pointing to the likeness on the front page of the newspaper.

"Why no," Snobbcraft lied, "but—but it looks like me, doesn't it?"

"You're mighty right it does!" said Rev. McPhule, sternly, "and it *is* you, too!"

"No, no, no, that's not me," cried the president of the Anglo-Saxon Association.

"Yes it is," roared McPhule, as the crowd closed in on the two hapless men. "It's you and you're a nigger, accordin' to this here paper, an' a newspaper wouldn't lie." Turning to his followers he commanded, "Take 'em. They're niggers just as I thought. The Lord's will be done. Idea of niggers runnin' on th' Demmycratic ticket!"

The crowd came closer. Buggerie protested that he was really white but it was of no avail. The crowd had sufficient excuse for doing what they had wanted to do at first. They shook their fists in the two men's faces, kicked them, tore off their nondescript garments, searched their pockets and found cards and papers proving their identity, and but for the calmness and presence of mind of the Rev. McPhule, the True Faith Christ Lovers would have torn the unfortunate men limb from limb. The evangelist restrained the more hotheaded individuals and insisted that the ceremonies proceed according to time-honored custom.

So the impetuous yielded to wiser counsel. The two men, vociferously protesting, were stripped naked, held down by

husky and willing farm hands and their ears and genitals cut
off with jack knives amid the fiendish cries of men and
women. When this crude surgery was completed, some wag
sewed their ears to their backs and they were released and
told to run. Eagerly, in spite of their pain, both men tried to
avail themselves of the opportunity. Anything was better
than this. Staggering forward through an opening made in
the crowd, they attempted to run down the dusty road, blood
streaming down their bodies. They had only gone a few feet
when, at a signal from the militant evangelist, a half-dozen
revolvers cracked and the two Virginians pitched forward
into the dust amid the uproarious laughter of the congregation.

The preliminaries ended, the two victims, not yet dead,
were picked up, dragged to the stake and bound to it, back
to back. Little boys and girls gaily gathered excelsior, scrap
paper, twigs and small branches while their proud parents
fetched logs, boxes, kerosene and the staves from a cider barrel. The fuel was piled up around the groaning men until
only their heads were visible.

When all was in readiness, the people fell back and the
Rev. McPhule, as master of ceremonies, ignited the pyre. As
the flames shot upward, the dazed men, roused by the flames,
strained vainly at the chains that held them. Buggerie found
his voice and let out yelp after yelp as flames licked at his fat
flesh. The crowd whooped with glee and Rev. McPhule
beamed with satisfaction. The flames rose higher and completely hid the victims from view. The fire crackled merrily
and the intense heat drove the spectators back. The odor of
cooking meat permeated the clear, country air and many a
nostril was guiltily distended. The flames subsided to reveal
a red-hot stake supporting two charred hulks.

There were in the assemblage two or three whitened Negroes, who, remembering what their race had suffered in the
past, would fain have gone to the assistance of the two men
but fear for their own lives restrained them. Even so they

were looked at rather sharply by some of the Christ Lovers because they did not appear to be enjoying the spectacle as thoroughly as the rest. Noticing these questioning glances, the whitened Negroes began to yell and prod the burning bodies with sticks and cast stones at them. This exhibition restored them to favor and banished any suspicion that they might not be one-hundred-per-cent Americans.

When the roasting was over and the embers had cooled, the more adventurous members of Rev. McPhule's flock rushed to the stake and groped in the two bodies for skeletal souvenirs such as forefingers, toes and teeth. Proudly their pastor looked on. This was the crowning of a life's ambition. Tomorrow his name would be in every newspaper in the United States. God had indeed answered his prayers. He breathed again his thanks as he thrust his hand into his pocket and felt the soothing touch of the hundred-dollar bill he had extracted from Snobbcraft's pocket. He was supremely happy.

AND SO ON AND SO ON

Bias against paleness

In the last days of the Goosie administration, the Surgeon-General of the United States, Dr. Junius Crookman, published a monograph on the differences in skin pigmentation of the real whites and those he had made white by the Black-No-More process. In it he declared, to the consternation of many Americans, that in practically every instance the new Caucasians were from two to three shades lighter than the old Caucasians, and that approximately one-sixth of the population were in the first group. The old Caucasians had never been really white but rather were a pale pink shading down to a sand color and a red. Even when an old Caucasian contracted vitiligo, he pointed out, the skin became much lighter.

To a society that had been taught to venerate whiteness

for over three hundred years, this announcement was rather
staggering. What was the world coming to, if the blacks were
whiter than the whites? Many people in the upper class began
to look askance at their very pale complexions. If it were true
that extreme whiteness was evidence of the possession of
Negro blood, of having once been a member of a pariah
class, then surely it were well not to be so white!

Dr. Crookman's amazing brochure started the entire country to examining shades of skin color again. Sunday magazine supplements carried long articles on the subject from
the pens of hack writers who knew nothing whatever of pigmentation. Pale people who did not have blue eyes began to
be whispered about. The comic weeklies devoted special
numbers to the question that was on everyone's lips. Senator
Bosh of Mississippi, about to run again for office, referred
several times to it in the Congressional Record, his remarks
interspersed with "Applauses." A popular song, "Whiter
Than White," was being whistled by the entire nation. Among
the working classes, in the next few months, there grew up
a certain prejudice against all fellow workers who were exceedingly pale.

The new Caucasians began to grow self-conscious and
resent the curious gazes bestowed upon their lily-white countenances in all public places. They wrote indignant letters to
the newspapers about the insults and discriminations to
which they were increasingly becoming subjected. They protested vehemently against the effort on the part of employers
to pay them less and on the part of the management of public institutions to segregate them. A delegation that waited
upon President Goosie firmly denounced the social trend and
called upon the government to do something about it. The
Down-With-White-Prejudice-League was founded by one
Karl von Beerde, whom some accused of being the same
Doctor Beard who had, as a Negro, once headed the National
Social Equality League. Offices were established in the Times

Dubois

Square district of New York and the mails were soon laden with releases attempting to prove that those of exceedingly pale skin were just as good as anybody else and should not, therefore, be oppressed. A Dr. Cutten Prodd wrote a book proving that all enduring gifts to society came from those races whose skin color was not exceedingly pale, pointing out that the Norwegians and other Nordic peoples had been in savagery when Egypt and Crete were at the height of their development. Prof. Handen Moutthe, the eminent anthropologist (who was well known for his popular work on *The Sex Life of Left-Handed Morons among the Ainus*) announced that as a result of his long research among the palest citizens, he was convinced they were mentally inferior and that their children should be segregated from the others in school. Professor Moutthe's findings were considered authoritative because he had spent three entire weeks of hard work assembling his data. Four state legislatures immediately began to consider bills calling for separate schools for pale children. Bias in inverse form

Those of the upper class began to look around for ways to get darker. It became the fashion for them to spend hours at the seashore basking naked in the sunshine and then to dash back, heavily bronzed, to their homes, and, preening themselves in their dusky skins, lord it over their paler, and thus less fortunate, associates. Beauty shops began to sell face powders named *Poudre Nègre, Poudre le Egyptienne* and *L'Afrique.*

Mrs. Sari Blandine (formerly Mme. Sisseretta Blandish of Harlem), who had been working on a steam table in a Broadway Automat, saw her opportunity and began to study skin stains. She stayed away from work one week to read up on the subject at the Public Library and came back to find a recent arrival from Czecho-Slovakia holding down her job.

Mrs. Blandine, however, was not downhearted. She had the information and in three or four weeks' time she had a skin stain that would impart a long-wearing light-brown tinge to the pigment. It worked successfully on her young daughter; so successfully, in fact, that the damsel received a proposal of marriage from a young millionaire within a month after applying it.

Free applications were given to all of the young women of the neighborhood. Mrs. Blandine's stain became most popular and her fame grew in her locality. She opened a shop in her front room and soon had it crowded from morning till night. The concoction was patented as Blandine's Egyptienne Stain.

By the time President-Elect Hornbill was inaugurated, her Egyptienne Stain Shoppes dotted the country and she had won three suits for infringement of patent. Everybody that was anybody had a stained skin. A girl without one was avoided by the young men; a young man without one was at a decided disadvantage, economically and socially. A white face became startlingly rare. America was definitely, enthusiastically mulatto-minded.

Imitations of Mrs. Blandine's invention sprang up like weeds in a cemetery. In two years there were fifteen companies manufacturing different kinds of stains and artificial tans. At last, even the Zulu Tan became the vogue among the smart set and it was a common thing to see a sweet young miss stop before a show window and dab her face with charcoal. Enterprising resort keepers in Florida and California, intent on attracting the *haute monde*, hired naturally black bathing girls from Africa until the white women protested against the practice on the ground that it was a menace to family life.

One Sunday morning Surgeon-General Crookman, in looking over the rotogravure section of his favorite newspaper, saw a photograph of a happy crowd of Americans arrayed in the latest abbreviated bathing suits on the sands at Cannes. In the group he recognized Hank Johnson, Chuck Foster, Bunny Brown and his real Negro wife, former

Imperial Grand Wizard and Mrs. Givens and Matthew and Helen Fisher. All of them, he noticed, were quite as dusky as little Matthew Crookman Fisher, who played in a sandpile at their feet.

Dr. Crookman smiled wearily and passed the section to his wife.

ALSO AVAILABLE

THE BLACKER THE BERRY . . .
Wallace Thurman
Introduction by Allyson Hobbs

GOD'S TROMBONES
Seven Negro Sermons in Verse
James Weldon Johnson
Foreword by Maya Angelou
General Editor: Henry Louis Gates, Jr.

IOLA LEROY
Frances Ellen Watkins Harper
Introduction by Hollis Robbins
General Editor: Henry Louis Gates, Jr.

THE LIFE OF JOHN THOMPSON,
A FUGITIVE SLAVE
John Thompson
Edited by William L. Andrews
Introduction by William L. Andrews
General Editor: Henry Louis Gates, Jr.

THE LIGHT OF TRUTH:
Writings of an Anti-Lynching Crusader
Ida B. Wells
Edited with an Introduction and Notes
by Mia Bay
General Editor: Henry Louis Gates, Jr.

NOT WITHOUT LAUGHTER
Langston Hughes
Introduction by Angela Flournoy

PASSING
Nella Larsen
Introduction by Emily Bernard

THE PORTABLE CHARLES W.
CHESNUTT
Charles W. Chesnutt
Edited by William L. Andrews
Introduction by William L. Andrews
General Editor: Henry Louis Gates, Jr.

QUICKSAND
Nella Larsen
Introduction by Thadious M. Davis

THE SOULS OF BLACK FOLK
With "The Talented Tenth" and "The
Souls of White Folk"
W. E. B. Du Bois
Introduction by Ibram X. Kendi

TWELVE YEARS A SLAVE
Solomon Northup
Foreword by Steve McQueen
Introduction by Ira Berlin
Afterword by Henry Louis Gates, Jr.
General Editor: Henry Louis Gates, Jr.

PENGUIN CLASSICS

Ready to find your next great read? Let us help. Visit prh.com/nextread

emphasis on recurrence
of problems